"Thanks aga key card. **"It was a very nice evening.**

"My pleasure," Dexter said, his voice slightly husky as he gently removed the card from Faye's hand, keeping his gaze locked with hers as he unlocked her door. He took a step, one that put his body within inches of hers; he was so close that she could feel his heat, imagine his "intention."

"Okay, so, good night." She averted her eyes and held out her hand. *Please! Just give me my key card before I die!*

But, no, that would have been too much like right. He had to place one hand on her shoulder and another on her chin, and turn her head ever so slightly. Then, he had to run his hand down her arm as he lowered his head and placed a kiss—soft and feathery—on her parted lips.

"Good night, Doctor," he murmured.

"Good night." She walked into the room, offered as best a smile as she could muster under the circumstances—keeping her knees from buckling and her heart from beating out her chest—and closed the door.

Inside the room, silence enveloped her. That…and abject loneliness unlike any she'd ever felt. She leaned against the door, took several calming breaths and asked herself the million-dollar question. *What. Just. Happened?*

Books by Zuri Day

Harlequin Kimani Romance

Diamond Dreams
Champagne Kisses
Platinum Promises

ZURI DAY

snuck her first Harlequin romance at the age of twelve from her older sister's off-limits collection and was hooked from page one. Knights in shining armor and happily-ever-afters filled her teen years and spurred a lifelong love of reading. That she now creates these stories as a full-time, award-winning author is a dream come true! Splitting her time between the stunning Caribbean islands and Southern California, she's always busy writing her next novel. Zuri makes time to connect with readers and meet with book clubs. She'd love to hear from you, and personally answers every email that's sent to Zuri@ZuriDay.com.

PLATINUM
Promises

ZURI DAY

HARLEQUIN® KIMANI™ ROMANCE

In love, a promise is a beautiful token

When heartfelt words are lovingly spoken

And there's magic when a partner makes a platinum vow

So amazing that the only response is…wow!

Recycling programs
for this product may
not exist in your area.

ISBN-13: 978-0-373-86305-1

PLATINUM PROMISES

HARLEQUIN®
www.Harlequin.com

Printed in U.S.A.

Dear Reader,

Platinum is one of the rarest elements on earth: exceptionally resistant and highly valuable. I believe the same can be said about the love between Dexter and Faye. Like platinum, he is lustrous—polished, dazzling—while her malleability during years spent doctoring in third-world countries has served her well. The rarity is in these two opposites attracting; the resiliency and value is a sustainable relationship formed on common ground.

Faye returns to the States from Port au Prince, Haiti, the capital city of the Western Hemisphere's poorest country, which was devastated by an earthquake in 2010. She reminds us that all these years later, much restorative work is still desperately needed. There are several charitable organizations through which we can pitch in and help, either by offering our time and services, as Faye did, or by making monetary contributions, Dexter-style.

Either way, for both this couple and for Haiti, love wins!

Zuri Day

Thanks to Glenda Howard and Harlequin's "Team Zuri"—especially Mr. IT (wink)—for being wonderful and fabulous. Because you are...I am!

Chapter 1

Practical, no-nonsense Dr. Faye Buckner lay in uncharted waters—literally and figuratively—feeling wanton, wicked and strangely...free. The water swirled around her body as her lover's tongue traced circles against her heartbeat, causing flutters from her stomach to her heat. *Ah, yes. The beautiful beaches of Haiti. But how did I get here with him?*

"Relax." Her lover's voice was as soothing as the water and as warm as a summer breeze.

"I can't."

"Yes, you can. I'll help you." He laid a trail of kisses down her neck, over her collarbone and on her shoulder, all the while brushing feathery fingers up and down her arm. Goosebumps appeared on the upper part of her body. A furnace of passion exploded within. He captured a nipple with his teeth, pulled it inside his mouth. Not wanting to appear rude or neglectful, he slid his hand to her other nipple, pebbling it between his thumb and forefinger before moving his hand down farther…to her navel, hip and inner thigh.

A foreign feeling of losing control caused her to squeeze her legs together.

Her lover raised up on one elbow as his finger slid up and down the crease caused by her tightly clenched thighs. She closed her eyes.

"Don't be shy," he said with a chuckle. "Trust me."

He leaned over and placed a soft, reverent kiss just below her navel.

Her breath came fast, and her heart beat faster.

He eased back up to her breast. Feathery kisses rained down on her dewy, soft skin, a trail of tantalizing sensations across the fleshy plains of her softness, her boyishly lean frame a perfect canvas for his oral artistry. He reached the thighs, which were still pressed against each other. He lowered himself farther, kissing, rubbing and licking the line that served as the gateway to her desire.

"Let go."

She moaned, shaking her head from side to side. She couldn't. She wouldn't! But why not? She had no answer to that question. Her mind was muddled, logic elusive. *How can this be happening?* But it was. She could feel it, could feel him, everywhere.

"Don't think, baby. Just feel. Give yourself to me." His tongue stiffened, became more insistent even as he eased his hands underneath her booty, licking a wedge between her armor, causing her thighs to part of their own volition. The act was unexpected, the air against her love button a delicious friction. *How is the wind blowing there?* She dared open one eye and look downward. His bow-shaped lips were parted; it was he who fanned her flame. There, in the most intimate of places. Hot breath touched her feminine furnace as he spread her legs and then kissed her inner thighs. Before she could ponder the deliciousness of the way his skillful tongue felt against her sensitive skin, he moved on to an even more sensitive spot and kissed it. She gasped, taking in a mouthful of air, releasing a lifetime of inhibitions. Without waiting for instruction or permission, her hips began a circular dance, lifting up to meet his tongue. Again, her rational self tried to intervene, tried to argue that such gyrations were inappropriate, lewd, nasty.

He licked her there. Between her lower lips. Once. Again. Deeper still. Reason fled, replaced by desire. She moaned, stroked his close-cropped hair as he stroked her.

"That's right. Relax and enjoy this." He ran his lips over her nether ones, over and again, kissing her with a tenderness that brought tears to her eyes and wetness in other places. She tossed and turned and tried to get away. He captured her thighs with his large hands, looked up at her with glazed eyes and a wicked smile. "You're not going anywhere," he said. "And neither am I."

In that moment, Faye's heart burst—and her head fell against something hard like steel, cold like glass and… leathery. Leather? At the ocean?

WTH?

The cheerful, gray-haired driver glanced back at his passenger waking from an unexpected nap. "Wake up, Sleeping Beauty. We're almost there!"

Chapter 2

Faye looked around, dazed and confused. She eyed palm trees and grapevines and signs announcing concerts and spas and wine tastings. Slowly the dream faded. Reality crashed in. She wasn't lying on a beach in Haiti. She was riding in the back of a town car on America's West Coast, not at all surprised that she'd been lulled to sleep during the one hour drive from San Diego International Airport to her destination, Temecula, California, the area she'd only recently learned was Southern California's wine country, even older than the more widely known Napa Valley. There had been little sleep in the past seventy-two hours, spent in what had been her home away from home for the past three years.

The memory of that beloved country brought a pang to her heart. She missed Haiti already. Or was it the lover in her dream that she longed for, and the fact that he was not real that made her sad? She narrowed her eyes, tried to "see" the man who'd taken her places she'd never been in waking moments. But there was no recalling his face. Only that body, hard and strong. Only the way he made her temperature soar, causing her to feel embarrassed as the driver looked into the rearview mirror and offered a fatherly smile.

"Looks like you're in for a treat," he said, turning onto a winding road bordered by Bird of Paradise bushes and fields of grapevines beyond them. "I wish the wife and I could afford to stay at a place like this."

"It does look beautiful," Faye agreed. She was immediately struck with how diametrically opposite her current surroundings were compared with those she'd seen mere hours ago. *Ian told me this place was like heaven. He was right.* Dr. Ian Chappelow was a philanthropist, mentor and friend. He was the reason why she was no longer in Haiti, the reason why she would see her lifelong dream come true—opening the Hearts of Health and Healing Center, a free clinic for poor families—and the reason why she was getting ready to step into the lobby area of California's award-winning Drake Wines Resort and Spa. Thinking of him reminded her that between the lengthy customs process and jet lag she'd forgotten to turn on her phone and "ring Haiti as soon as I arrive stateside," as she'd promised.

The driver opened her door. Faye stepped out and walked around to the trunk of the vehicle, fully prepared to grab her bags.

"Oh, no, miss," the driver said, easily pulling her two pieces of luggage out and closing the trunk. "I'll take these to the front desk for you or, if you prefer, to the bell captain to be delivered to your room."

"Of course." Faye nodded, granting the driver a brief, bright smile. "It's been a while since I've been catered to in this way. The front desk will be fine. I can handle them from there. Thank you."

"No problem, miss." The driver walked with her into the hotel and up to the check-in counter.

Faye dug into her oversized canvas bag for her wallet. "How much do I owe you?"

The driver held up his hands with a smile. "Everything has already been taken care of, including the tip. I hope you enjoy your stay."

That rascal. Ian had already given her more than she'd ever dreamed possible. She'd insisted that he do nothing more regarding her vacation than pay for the hotel. *I see how he listened. Not at all!* Faye thanked the driver and within minutes was checked in by the cheery brunette who'd welcomed her to the "Inland Escape," a tag that she'd later learn had been created by the resort's director of PR. She accepted her key cards, secured a carry-on handle in each hand and headed toward the bank of elevators the receptionist had indicated. Even in her exhausted state she took in the eclectic yet perfect mix of marble and bamboo, silk walls and bronze fixtures. When scanning the brochures describing the resort, Faye had noted its exclusive feel and had mentioned to Ian her concern at the expense of this trip. "You deserve it," he'd told her with a reassuring squeeze of her shoulder. "You're a tireless worker who refuses to rest. Besides, it feels good spending money on the daughter I never had. Those two heathen sons of mine are chomping at the bit to get my fortune after I die." Faye had shushed talk of death and heathens with an "I love you, Doctor" and a heartfelt hug. Now, looking around, it was clear that the doctor had indeed spent a good sum of money on his "adopted" child.

Halfway across the lobby, Faye walked too close to a vase-holding table, causing her carry-on to get caught in its legs. The stuck luggage was wrenched out of her hands, and the unexpected imbalance caused Faye to stumble. *Geez!* Having carried bags across rougher terrain, Faye knew that exhaustion was to blame for her errant strides. And she knew just the prescription to help her feel better: sleep. She quickly righted herself, freed the luggage and took three more steps toward the bank of elevators before she looked up, saw a vision and for a second wondered if she'd stepped back into her dream. She hadn't recalled the face of the phantom man who'd played her body like an instrument while she was sleeping, but if she had, she was sure that he would look like the one across the way, brow creased in concentration as a thumb lazily rubbed the face of a cell phone, the other hand in his pocket.

Eyes trained to take in surroundings and/or symptoms in an instant registered his information on a mental chart: six-one or two, maybe one eighty-five, gorgeous. She could see only his side profile, but if it were any indication of what a full frontal looked like, then Lord. Have. Mercy. Even from the side she could see an aquiline nose, thick lips and a strong brow. Her glances were quick, surreptitious, taking in what had to be a tailored suit; the well-fitted jacket lay across broad shoulders and fell over lean hips. His legs were long, his feet were...*don't go there, Faye. Seriously! That dream has you feeling all beside yourself!* While in the jungles of Africa or the makeshift shanties of Port-au-Prince, it had been easy to forget how long she'd gone without a date, let alone an intimate evening. Burying herself in work had kept thoughts of romance at bay; eighteen-hour days had made sleep her only desire when she fell into bed. But the dream had reminded her of what she'd been missing—no, of what she'd never experienced. She wasn't a virgin, but Faye was positive that she'd never been loved like that, had never experienced what had transpired in her dream. Those sure hands, that skilled tongue…*stop it!* Even as she worked to divert her train of thought to a subject less…volatile…an involuntary shiver went through her body. She reached the bank of elevators, pushed the button and vowed to herself that she would not look back, that she wouldn't take one last look at that delectable dish of dark caramel. She argued with herself that it would be senseless to gaze upon that sculpted body just one last time, to commit it to memory, to invite him into her subconscious, and perhaps another passion-filled dream. *Faye Buckner, pull yourself together. You are not having that kind of dream ever again! And you're not going to look at him.* Only her head didn't get the memo, as seemingly of its own will it turned in the direction of the human god. Her eyes betrayed her as well, quickly finding the object of her desire. When they did, it was to find that the man she'd already unconsciously dubbed "the man of her dreams" had finished his scrolling or texting or whatever and was looking in her direction. *Is he looking at me? No, couldn't be. Torn jeans. Ratty T-shirt. I'd hardly garner his attention.* And then he smiled. And winked. At her, *definitely* at her. *And since you can see him looking at you, Faye, then he is undoubtedly very aware that you are staring at him.*

Crap! Faye quickly turned away, wishing upon ten thousand stars that the elevator would come now, that the doors would open up and rescue her from this extreme embarrassment. At that second, the chime of the bell announced her chariot's arrival. It couldn't have been more welcomed had it been Peter's blowing horn announcing that she'd been accepted through heaven's pearly gates. She hurried into the elevator and turned to smile at the handsome stranger, whom she assumed from his attire had conducted business at the hotel and was someone she'd more than likely not see again. Her smile quickly flitted away, however, as she saw a laughing, dark-skinned beauty walk up to him and lean in for a hug. He kissed her cheek. The doors closed. Her heart dropped. *Of course he's taken. Someone who looks like that wouldn't be spending his nights alone.* And then the next thought. *What do you care?* A useless feeling, really, although somehow it mattered. And considering her third thought, Faye knew that it shouldn't matter. Not at all. *He was flirting with me while waiting for her? What a jerk!* It was just as well. Whatever fantasy she'd created in the seconds she'd seen him needed to fade away just as quickly as her dream had. She hadn't come back to the United States to flirt or date or play footsy with some heartthrob. She'd come here to realize an entirely different type of dream: opening a free clinic in a poverty-stricken area of San Diego, to develop a model that would hopefully be re-created in inner cities across the country, and to make her friend, mentor and millionaire who was largely funding her endeavor, Dr. Ian Chappelow, proud.

This place indeed looks magical but you are not Cinderella, this is no fairy tale and that oh-so-gorgeous, dimpled piece of corporate goodness is not your Prince Charming. Period. End of story.

She reached the room boasting the number on the card envelope she'd been given, opened the door and stopped short. Convincing herself that she wasn't in a fairy tale while staying in these surroundings would not be easy to do. She stepped inside, closed the door and did a slow 360-degree turn. The suite was straight out of a magazine or movie screen. Ian had booked her in a suite, and the living and dining areas alone looked incredibly impressive. The floors were a dark-colored polished wood, the couch and loveseat the color of rose wine. A beautiful multicol-

ored rug anchored that area and complemented the glass
and metal coffee and end tables. Beyond the living room
was the dining room, complete with buffet. The open-concept kitchen was small yet highly functional, its stainless-
steel appliances gleaming in the afternoon sun. Walking
to the oversized, floor-to-ceiling windows, Faye beheld
the most beautifully landscaped garden she had ever seen.
There was a profusion of flowers, perfectly-formed shrub-
bery and a large fountain in the middle. The cobblestone
path added a classic touch to the modern architecture. The
mountains soared toward the brilliant blue sky.

"Are you *sure* you're not Cinderella?" she mumbled.
Wow, Ian...thanks. She continued to gaze out the window,
overcome with emotion for the man who'd helped her become a better doctor, had helped her realize her dreams
and had sent her here. Batting away tears and battling emotions from she knew not what, she reached for her phone
and dialed Ian's cell phone. The call went to voicemail. She
left a brief message, plopped down on the bed and fought
off a wave of melancholy.

"You're exhausted, Doctor. You need sleep and a
shower." *And not necessarily in that order.*

She walked into the oversized bathroom, stripped off
her clothes and stepped into the marble shower. Her goals
were to rinse off the weariness and the grime from her
journey—and to hopefully wash away her gloominess as
well. But as she brushed the loofah sponge over her body,
images of sexy eyes and succulent lips, of broad shoulders
and long, lean legs flitted across her mind's eye. She tried
to tell herself it was the man from her dream. But, no. The
person she was envisioning was all too real. The type of
man that women like Faye could only dream about. The
type that beautiful women dated, and lucky women married. Like the woman in the lobby, perhaps, the woman

whom the man of her dreams had kissed on the cheek. Of course he'd be attracted to someone sexy and flawless. Not someone like her.

Chapter 3

"I saw you!" Marissa Drake said after their greeting, eyeing her brother-in-law with playful suspicion.

"What?"

"Dexter Drake! Don't even try it. I saw you looking at and flirting with the woman who was waiting by the elevator."

"Who? The toned, natural-looking sister, about five seven or eight, with the long legs and cute tush? Naw, I wasn't looking at her."

"Right. You weren't paying her any attention at *all*." They laughed as Marissa hooked her arm through his and they began walking toward the hotel entrance. Even before marrying Dexter's brother, Donovan, a year ago, she and the youngest Drake had developed a special bond. Part of it was his effervescent personality, and part of it was the fact that when both Donovan and Marissa were trying to deny their mutual attraction, Dexter forced his brother's

hand by jokingly implying he was interested in Marissa.
He'd threatened to ask her out if Donovan didn't. That had
led to a scowling "don't you dare" from his more reserved
brother followed by a campaign from Donovan for Marissa's love that would have impressed a presidential candi-
date. Marissa thought about a particular conversation that
took place during this time, and chuckled.

"What's funny?"

"Nothing, just thinking." An improbable thought came
to her mind, but she dismissed it immediately. Dexter may
be a matchmaker. She was not. Besides, Dexter liked sultry, flashy women. The woman at the elevator did not at
all look his type. "So...what has a Drake Wines executive
pulling kitchen duty on a Thursday afternoon?"

"Huh? Oh, right." Dexter knew that one could see the
door to the kitchen when sitting at the end of the bar. Marissa had obviously seen him exit it. "I was meeting with
the chef to make sure that everything is in place for Papa's
party tomorrow." David Drake Sr., Dexter's great-grandfather, whom everyone affectionately called Papa Dee, had
been born on the sprawling, mountainous land inherited
by *his* grandfather almost two centuries ago. His centenary
celebration would be the resort's highlight of the month.
"The kitchen staff is as excited as the rest of us and has
done a bang-up job."

"I'm really looking forward to the party. It's going to be
wonderful to pay tribute to Papa Dee in this way."

"What about you? What had you sipping wine at the
bar on a Thursday?"

"On my way back from Riverside and decided to drop
by."

"What's going on in Riverside?"

"A good friend of mine recently divorced and moved
back there. I went to help her settle in and offer moral sup-

port. I'd thought about meeting Don here, maybe having dinner with the in-laws. But when I reached him he reminded me about the meeting he had with your cousin."

Dexter smiled at the mention of his cousin, Warren Drake, part of the clan formerly known as the Drakes of Louisiana. Several years ago, four of the six brothers in that family had relocated to Northern California, when gold had been discovered on land that had been in their family for decades. The siblings had incorporated the land, founded a town and were soon movers and shakers in Paradise Valley, California. Most of the Drakes of Louisiana were now the Drakes of California, just like their cousins. They were also smart and shrewd with business savvy, which is why Donovan was meeting with Warren—to expand their businesses and their brands.

They exited the hotel. "So…what does your friend look like?" Dexter asked. "Is she fine?"

Marissa gave Dexter the side eye. "You are not interested. She has four children."

"Whoa!"

"Ha! Thought that would make you put that player card back in your pocket. Everyone knows you're allergic to kids."

"That's not true. Kids are cool…as long as they're not mine."

"So everything is set for Papa Dee's party?" Marissa asked, clearly not up for a debate on the value of anyone's next generation and changing the subject to prove it.

Dexter nodded. "Because of the RSVPs and sold-out rooms, we had to expand the menu, but I consider that a good problem to have. They are working hard to make sure his favorite dishes are executed to perfection."

"What about the cake?"

"That's being done by an outside company, one that

specializes in imaging. It will feature a picture of Papa, set against a vineyard backdrop, with one hundred candles lighting the way from the countryside to the hotel."

"Wow. Papa Dee is turning one hundred years old. I can't even imagine what it will feel like to be in this crazy world another seventy years."

"I can't imagine it either," Dexter said. "But I hope I get to experience it." They reached his car. "Where are you parked?"

"Not far."

"You want to ride to the house with me and join us for dinner, since Don is acting like the workaholic that he is?"

"Thanks, Dexter, but no. I think I'll head on home and make dinner for two."

"Listen to you sounding all domesticated."

"Marriage will do that to you," Marissa said with a laugh. "You ought to try it."

"Naw, I'm good."

"Are you sure?"

"Positive. You saw what happened to the last woman who tried to tie me down."

"I sure did, but I respect Maria. You can't be mad at a woman in her thirties who doesn't want to continue dating—" Marissa used air quotes "—for the next ten years."

Dexter opened his car door. "On that female-biased note, I'm out."

"Ha! Whatever."

"I'll see you at the party tomorrow."

"See you."

Dexter slid into the soft leather seat of his latest toy and made the five-minute trip from the boutique hotel that anchored the resort to the Drake estate to have dinner with his parents. On the way, he thought about what Marissa had said. In two short years both of his older siblings had found their true loves and married them. As a result, his sister, Diamond, had blossomed into an even more beautiful and confident woman with a child on the way, and his brother, Donovan, was happier than Dexter had ever remembered.

"But that's not you, man," Dexter said aloud as he pulled into the circular drive of the family home, where he still lived. "There are too many clusters on the vine for you to be satisfied with just one grape."

Chapter 4

Faye was startled awake, this time by her ringing cell phone. She looked at the clock on her nightstand in amazement, checked that time against what was shown on her watch. What had been intended as a five-minute nap before ordering room service had turned into the first seven uninterrupted hours of sleep she'd had in a very long time. Before, when she'd worked in Africa, and for the past three years that she'd spent in Haiti, four to five hours of sleep per night was the norm, six or seven a luxury. She yawned, stretched and reached for her phone, smiling as she rapidly typed out a text to Ian:

I called and left a message, but here's a text as well. The brochures don't do it justice, Doctor! This place is more beautiful than I could have imagined. I plan to enjoy every minute here, and will call you tomorrow. Again, thanks so much.

Eleven-thirty here, Faye thought. *That means it's two-*

thirty in Haiti. Faye wanted to talk to her best friend, Adeline Marceaux, a native who served as director of Haitian Heartbeats, the organization through which many doctors, including Faye, had entered the country following a devastating earthquake. "She might be up, but I shouldn't chance it," Faye said to herself. *I'll just call her tomorrow.*

As she placed the phone on the nightstand, it rang. "I don't believe it!" she exclaimed, looking at the number. "Hello?" The voice on the other end was a bit distorted. Faye pressed the phone against her ear, trying to hear more clearly. "Addie?"

"Faye! Can you hear me?"

"Yes! It's a little scratchy, but that's okay."

"Hold on a minute." Faye heard a rustling sound, a closing door and then Adeline's voice, loud and clear.

"Is this better?"

"I can hear you just fine. Girl, you are going to live a long time," Faye said, a phrase she'd heard the islanders use when someone you were just thinking about got in touch. "I just thought about calling you but figured it was too late."

"You know how it is—our work is never done."

"Where are you?"

"Home, now. We just returned from the backcountry," Adeline explained in the lyrical accent that Faye adored. "Delivering food, water and emergency supplies to some families there. The rains are supposed to begin tomorrow in earnest. We wanted to make sure these provisions were delivered before the roads washed out."

"I miss Haiti already and wish I were there to help."

"Don't worry about us. You are exactly where you need to be, which I assume is the resort. Did you arrive safely?"

"I did." Faye described what she had seen so far.

"Sounds lovely. Reminds me of a hotel I visited in Saint Thomas."

Faye stood and began meandering around the room as she talked. "What about the new volunteers? Was their plane able to land?"

"Yes, and you'd like them. One is from Sweden, the grandson of one of Dr. Ian's friends. The other is a young medical student from Nigeria. Brilliant. Lots of ideas that he learned while helping orphans in the Sudan."

"Sounds like the kind of help I could use at my clinic."

"Perhaps. But you're not supposed to be thinking about work right now. You're supposed to be relaxing and taking advantage of the amenities that I'm sure are at your fingertips."

"I know. I'll try. But I'm so excited about how plans for the clinic are coming together, even though there is still so much to do. The contractor we hired for renovations fell through. He has to be replaced ASAP. Then there are the in-person interviews with the candidates honed from the online résumés received, meetings with the public relations firm and prepping for the benefit fundraiser. Through the churches, shelters and other organizations working with the clinic, there are already almost a hundred children to be screened. I can already use another doctor on board and the nursing staff—"

"Faye!" Adeline's voice was loud and firm.

"I know," Faye said with a self-conscious chuckle. "I should be relaxing." She noticed an envelope that had been slid under the door, and picked it up. "But it's so hard to turn off, you know?"

"You are a compassionate, dedicated doctor. You give and give until there is nothing left. Now is *your* time, Faye. For the next week, be a little selfish. Pamper yourself. Get a massage, a mani/pedi…find a cute guy who can knock the cobwebs out of those seldom-used girlie parts."

"Seriously, Adeline! You did not just go there."

"Ha! I most certainly did. You've gone far too long without the love of a man. It's time for you to get back in the dating game and find someone to make you happy."

"I'm already happy," Faye murmured, opening the elegant-looking linen envelope and pulling out the gold-embossed card.

"Then find someone with whom to share that happiness. Go flirt with a man, girl!"

A vision immediately came to mind—the man from the lobby, the man of her dreams. *The man who was last seen kissing a beautiful woman, Faye. Don't forget that.*

"Faye, are you listening?"

"Actually, I was reading an invitation from the resort. It must have been placed under my door while I napped."

"What does it say?"

"It says…

Drake Wines Resort and Spa invites you to join in the celebration of its founder, David "Papa Dee" Drake, Sr., as he marks his 100th birthday!

When: Friday, August 8, @ 5:00 p.m.

Where: Gardens of the South Lawn

There will be food, fun and, of course, Southern California's finest wines!

RSVP recommended, but not required."

"There you go, girl," Adeline squealed, the smile in her voice reaching through the phone. "An invitation to a party. Perfect! Go and buy yourself something sexy, put on some heels and flirt with every man in the room. Have some fun, Doctor. That's an order!"

After ending the call, Faye ordered from the twenty-four-hour room service menu. Thirty minutes later she enjoyed an all-American hamburger and fries, washing it down with a classic cola. She turned on the television and tried to focus on an over-the-top show about hip-hop artists in Atlanta, Georgia, and the women who loved them. Her eyes were on the screen, but her thoughts were on cobwebs, girlie parts, one certain businessman…and a dream.

Chapter 5

Because of the long nap, it had been almost 3 a.m. before Faye had settled into slumber. She woke up, sat up against the headboard and looked around. It was ten o'clock in the morning and she had no patients to see, no chores to do, no visits to make to tent villages and no idea what one did with idle time. It occurred to her that because her job was also her passion, she'd not taken a true vacation in almost five years. *What do people do all day when they have nothing to do?* She eyed the remote on the nightstand next to her, picked it up and turned on the large, flat-screen TV. After watching the infomercial on Drake Wines, she flipped through the channels. Five minutes and she knew that watching actors she did not know and shows she did not understand would not be how she spent her spare time. She turned off the television and tossed down the remote. *Now what?*

She looked around the luxurious, perfectly appointed

room. Her eye landed on the envelope with *You're invited* across the front. "The party," she murmured, picking up the card once again. *Maybe I should take Addie's advice and attend. But what would I wear?* After several years in Africa, and three years in Haiti, her wardrobe had been reduced to khakis, jeans and one simple black dress that she'd worn to the rare formal dinner. *Go and buy yourself something sexy, put on some heels and flirt with every man in the room.* "Addie is right. I should try and have fun." That decided, Faye scheduled a massage, a mani/pedi and an appointment at the salon, then ordered a rental car through the concierge. By the time she showered, dressed and did a quick online search, her car was downstairs. With one last look around the room she headed to the elevators, reached the shiny rental, programmed the car's GPS and set out for something she hadn't seen in about a year—a shopping mall.

As she listened to the female voice of the GPS telling her to turn left and right, she continued thinking about her conversation with Adeline about her love life. Or, more correctly, her lack thereof. During high school she'd been a bookworm and a loner with no real friends. That changed in college when she found herself surrounded by people who were as geeky as she was, who felt that devouring books and obsessing over studying were the most natural things to do in the world. That's where she'd met Jesse, a biochemical major. They dated until she began med school. He took a high-paying job in Alaska. Their romance couldn't survive the distance.

It was all about the career until the Peace Corps, where she'd met Phillip, a studious yet sensitive chap from Birmingham, England. Drawn together by their mutual desire to heal the world, Faye thought she'd found her soul mate. Unfortunately, when she received the inner call to help the earthquake victims of Haiti, Phillip didn't get that message. They vowed to keep in touch. He promised to visit. Neither happened. Another relationship gone.

And finally, Gerald McPherson. Older man. Brilliant doctor. Faye had been all agog. But Gerald hadn't a clue. He viewed her as a little sister, and rather than risk being hurt or embarrassed, she hid her crush behind a professional veneer. Good thing too because a year after he'd arrived in Africa he got a visit from his high school sweetheart. Three months later he went back to the States and married her.

Faye reached the mall and began a methodical walk through the stores. Maybe she shouldn't have spent so much time thinking about exes and unavailable loves. Because now she doubted her ability to take her friend's advice and have a good time.

"Looking good there, Papa!" Dexter strolled into his great-grandfather's bedroom, where a barber had just finished giving Papa Dee a haircut and a facial. "You're going to have the ladies fighting over you."

"Won't be the first time," Papa Dee drawled.

"Ha!"

The barber chuckled, too. "Again, happy birthday, Mr. Drake," he said, packing up his equipment. Dexter paid him and showed him to the door.

When he returned to the room, Papa Dee asked, "Did you invite Charlotte, the woman from the casino that I told you about?" His breathing was a little labored, but his eyes twinkled.

"Sure did. But somebody else invited themselves."

Papa Dee shook his head. "That Birdie needs to get a life."

"Aw, come on now, Pops. You've known Miss Birdie for what…about thirty years?"

"Yep. And that's about twenty-nine too many." Papa Dee eyed himself in the mirror, turning this way and that.

"He did a great job," Dexter said, watching his great-grandfather in the mirror. "You look good."

"Not bad for an old geezer."

"You're going to be the best looking man in the place."

"I will so long as you stay out of the room."

"Couldn't have been me if there hadn't been you. Here," Dexter said, walking over to the garment bag that hung in the closet. "Look what I bought you." He unzipped it to reveal a lightweight, ivory-colored summer suit paired with a tan shirt and striped tie. "You're going to be killing 'em, player!"

"If we're talking about Birdie, she's near 'bout dead already. One foot in the grave and the other on a piece of ice."

"Don't be so hard on her, Pops. I think she looks good for her age."

"Anybody seventy-five and still aboveground looks good! She's too old for me. I told her that!"

Dexter hid a smile. "I know, Papa. But somehow she knew about the party. Mom couldn't uninvite her."

"I'll handle it," Papa said with a sigh, spoken like one who more than once had had experience in this area. "Now, that Charlotte…"

"I can't argue with you, Papa. She's got it going on for sure." She was also forty-five *going on* forty-six. But somehow Papa Dee had finagled her number and they'd been meeting to play bingo at the casino for the past two months.

"You always want to pick somebody who can stoke your fire, son, someone who'll get your willy working, make you want to run a mile over hot coals…in bare feet!"

"Man, you're a mess." Dexter looked at his watch. "We

should probably get you ready." Papa Dee balanced his hands on both arms of the chair before standing. He took a step and stumbled slightly. "Papa?" Dexter was over in an instant. "Are you all right?"

"Fine, I'm fine." Papa Dee waved him away. "All of this fussing over me has my head in a swoon."

"You sure you haven't snuck into some of that brandy you've been distilling? I noticed that someone had been in an area of the cellar where only two people have the key."

"Only two people that you know of," Papa Dee answered...without answering. "There'll be plenty of time for spirits. But for me to manage all of these women this evening, I've got to have my head on right."

Chapter 6

Before turning the corner, Faye heard the music, laughter and chatter of a party in full swing. She slowed just for a moment, running her hand across her abdomen to quiet the butterflies. In doing so she noted the softness of her newly purchased sundress's fabric and the way the extra material swirled around her ankles. Bared arms wouldn't have been her first choice. But when the boutique worker saw Faye's toned body she'd gone immediately to the form-fitting floral number, and once seeing her in it had suggested a pair of strappy sandals with three-inch heels. Faye had appreciated her clerk-slash-stylist and had purchased those items, adding a lightweight shawl and jewelry to match. She had promised to return the following week to further update her wardrobe. She'd returned to the hotel just in time for the died-and-gone-to-heaven massage that was followed by the manicure, pedicure and salon visit.

"A haircut please, very close to the scalp," she'd told the receptionist once she'd stepped inside.

Her beautician had other plans. "You have such a nice grade of hair," she'd said, running her hands through Faye's one-inch curls. "I could condition it and treat it so that ringlets form. With the shape of your face, it would look wonderful."

"I'm not up for high maintenance," Faye had countered.

"It's a wash-and-go style, guaranteed."

When Faye had returned to the room and taken the time to really study her reflection in the mirror—new hairstyle and, thanks to the threaded brow arch and mud mask treatment she'd gotten, new face—she hardly recognized herself. Now, teetering on heels she rarely wore and heading into a crowd of people she didn't know…she again wondered who'd entered her body and where was the doctor whose idea of fun was poring over periodicals of the latest medical breakthrough. *This is all your fault, Addie! And I'd like to take a scalpel to the one who invented heels!*

"The party can't start until you join us." Faye's breath caught as the words delivered by a sexy, masculine voice seemed to pour into her ear from much too close a distance. She smelled sandalwood and cedar and felt her stomach flop. "You were heading into the party, correct?"

She dared a glance. Big mistake. *Oh, my God, it's him!* The businessman-slash-jerk, she told herself, who'd openly flirted with her while his wife-slash-date-slash-whomever was close by. "Actually," she began, in her most authoritative voice, "I was…" He stepped directly in front of her, forcing eye contact, "deciding…whether or not…um…" So much for hiding behind a professional veneer. Eight years of schooling, two degrees and an M.D. behind her name, yet suddenly she'd lost command of the King's English.

"You've got to come to this celebration. I insist. You'll be the prettiest flower in the garden." The handsome stranger placed a hand under her elbow and gently propelled her forward. "My name is Dexter," he said, as they walked. "Friends call me Dex."

"Faye Buckner." She took a breath, and then another, and then wondered about the woman he'd kissed yesterday afternoon. How did she find out? Just ask him outright? *Boy, am I rusty on dating decorum and social protocol.* She decided to say nothing, for now.

Dexter stopped at an open bar that was just beyond the hedges that framed the garden's opening. "Would you like a glass of champagne?"

"Yes, thanks."

While Dexter placed the order, Faye was allowed a brief reprieve to look around and get her act together. Hard to do when in a fairy-tale garden, standing next to a prince and wearing a crystal-covered slipper, but she called on discipline honed in residency and gathered herself just in time to realize Dexter was asking a question.

"You arrived yesterday, right?"

"Yes."

"On vacation?"

"Yes." *Are you stuck on stupid or just on that word?!* Faye cleared her throat. "What about you? Here on business?"

"You could say that." Dexter smiled, and Faye noticed that sexy hint of a dimple in his left cheek. "I work here."

The bartender placed down their flutes. Dexter picked up one and gave it to Faye. "To a wonderful vacation in wine country," he said.

Faye nodded. "Cheers."

As she took her first sip, a pretty pregnant woman walked up to them. Faye immediately thought of the dark-skinned woman from yesterday and wondered where this expectant mother fit in the equation. She didn't have to wait long to find out.

"Brother!" the woman snapped as she reached them. "Excuse me," she said to Faye before turning her attention back on her intended target. "Where is your cell phone?"

Dexter's devil-may-care attitude never faltered. Nor did his smile. "Why are you being all fussy and looking evil? You need to chill and come to me correctly if you come at all." He turned to Faye. "She's usually not like this." Nodding toward her protruding stomach, he added, "Hormones, I'm told."

"Excuse me for not bowing down and genuflecting, Your Highness, but I have been dealing with the press and calling you, all while trying to divert a catastrophe. A minor sibling squabble," the woman said to Faye. "Please forgive us."

"If you haven't figured it out, this is my sister, Diamond," Dexter said, turning to Faye with a feigned look of chagrin. "She's normally in full use of her manners, but since Junior landed in her stomach it's scrambled her brain."

"Oh, shut up." Diamond gave Dexter a playful push. "Diamond Drake-Wright," she said with a smile and an extended hand. "I take it you're Dexter's date. You have my condolences."

"No, not his date," Faye managed to respond, shaking Diamond's hand even as her mind whirled. "I'm a guest." *Drake…Wright…as in the Drake in Drake Resorts?* Now it all made sense: his cockiness, the self-assuredness, almost to a fault. The brochure had stated this was Drake land for more than a hundred years. Dexter had grown up eating with a silver spoon. This paradise was his home; heaven…his backyard!

"Thanks for joining us. I hope you enjoy the party. If you'll excuse us, my brother is needed over at the production booth. You did bring the DVD, right?"

"Aw, man! I knew I was forgetting something. Excuse me," he said to Faye, and hurried off.

Diamond and Faye watched his retreating back in silence. "And he says my brain is scrambled." Diamond's was the voice of innocence. "Go figure." The ladies laughed. Diamond walked away, and for the first time since she'd heard his voice and smelled his scent...Faye exhaled.

Chapter 7

After a single glass of bubbly, the rare-drinking Faye was more relaxed and ready to mingle. She walked to one of the buffet stations, fixed a plate and was soon seated at a table that included a couple from England, two BFFs from Nebraska, a father and daughter celebrating her birthday and a businessman from Texas, complete with Stetson, boots and spurs. All the people at the table were friendly and their talkative natures made her feel comfortable. She'd just savored a spoonful of succulent gumbo when a man bearing a resemblance to Dexter spoke into the microphone.

"Good afternoon, everyone!"

His father perhaps? Faye placed down her spoon and listened.

"My name is David Drake Jr. I want to thank all of you for coming here today to celebrate the birthday of this resort's founder, my father, David Drake Sr. Today, he turns one-hundred years old!" The partygoers cheered and applauded. "As any of you who've had the pleasure of meeting him can imagine, the stories are many, the history vast. A detailed biography is included in the programs placed at each table setting and also available in the hotel lobby. For now, please enjoy this short documentary highlighting some of the rich and colorful history of this amazing man.

"As the film plays, the waitstaff will deliver glasses of champagne to every table. Please refrain from drinking them until the end of the film, where we will toast the man known fondly as…Papa Dee."

Along with the other almost five-hundred guests, Faye watched in part amazement, part amusement as the story of the life of Papa Dee unfolded in the seven-minute film. The family had managed to retain impeccably preserved pictures of Papa Dee during various stages of his life: from the twelve-year-old standing between his maternal French grandparents to the twenty-five-year-old standing with his first wife. Narrated by family members, the documentary blended history with humor and offered a snapshot into what the viewers concluded was a diverse and interesting life. As she watched the film, Faye also snuck peaks at the family Papa Dee built, the ones she knew. Dexter sat next to his great-grandfather, seeming to keep up a running dialogue as they both watched the film. At times, the older man chuckled. At others, he'd lean over to whisper into an attentive Dexter's ear. Faye found herself wishing she were a whisker on Papa's aged chin just to hear what transpired during those obviously treasured moments. Smiling at the tableau before her, she was totally caught off guard when Dexter looked up and caught her staring. *Busted!* She slid her eyes away from the pair, but not before noticing Dexter laugh at something the old man said, head thrown back, pearly whites sparkling, arm reaching across the chair to hug Papa Dee's slightly bent shoulders. *What does that feel like,* she wondered, *to have a family that is so successful, and so close?*

Faye wouldn't know. Not really, anyway. There were fond memories scattered here and there: a Christmas at SeaWorld in San Diego; Thanksgiving with her father's parents when she was seven. Her paternal grandparents lived on a farm in Tennessee. It was the first time she'd seen cows, chickens and pigs up close. But her father was a military man, army, gone from home a lot. During their many moves she gained a love for reading but made few friends. Her mother, an outgoing woman whose big personality often overshadowed her daughter, seemed content to leave Faye to her own devices while she either worked toward her BS in business management or socialized with the other wives, usually around a card game or television show. When she was eleven years old, her world got flipped upside down. The family moved to Saint Louis, Faye discovered a love for medicine and her life forever changed. Looking at Dexter's sister, Diamond, leaning against a tall, handsome man whom Faye presumed was her husband, along with a group of about ten other people Faye imagined were part of the Drake family, Faye felt an unfamiliar pang of longing for family…and for love.

The cheering crowd brought Faye out of her reverie, and belatedly she realized she'd missed the last part of the film. What she couldn't miss was six feet two inches of delectable goodness rising from his seat to take the mike.

"Hello, everyone. My name is Dexter, a fifth-generation Drake and the vintner here at Drake Wines Resort and Spa. In other words, under the watchful eye of the man we're celebrating, I developed the bubbly we're about to sip right now." He raised the flute in his hand to their laughter and applause. "And now, a few words from the man who taught me everything I know, the man of the hour…David 'Papa

Dee' Drake!" Everyone clapped again and turned their attention to Papa Dee.

When he stood, Faye noted that even with bent shoulders he stood tall. *Had to have been six one, six two in his heyday.* She realized that he and Dexter had the same eyes and nose. She also realized that she was spending way too much time analyzing all things Dexter Drake. Here it was almost six o'clock in the afternoon and she hadn't thought about the clinic she was building or Haitian Heartbeats all day!

As one by one people rose to their feet, Papa Dee stood before the crowd with teary eyes. "Papa Dee Drake! Papa Dee Drake!" they chanted, and Faye joined in. Papa Dee waved his hands to quiet the crowd. "I appreciate all of the love that y'all are showing me. It's true I'm no longer a spring chicken. But I'm not a cooked goose either!" The audience roared. "Thank you!"

Papa Dee sat, and another man stood up and addressed the crowd. "My name is Donald Drake, president and chief operating officer of the resort and proud grandson of David Drake Sr. Everyone, please, let's sing 'Happy Birthday' to Papa Dee and then raise our glasses in a unanimous toast!"

The song was sung, the toast was made and soon the covered patio was filled with those dancing to some of Papa Dee's favorite songs. Dexter was the first one out on the dance floor, twirling a vivacious Latina to a fast-paced "Minnie the Moocher." It wasn't long, however, before a Tyra look-alike tapped Ms. Latina on the shoulder. Dexter didn't miss a beat as the "Moocher" segued into "A Tisket, A Tasket." They kicked and stomped and step-ball-changed across the dance floor before he spun her away with one arm and pulled in his sister with the other. The siblings took a trip on the A train, and when they stopped the band had gone from the forties to the fifties without missing a beat. Chuck Berry, Elvis Presley and Ray Charles hits kept the dance floor packed, but Faye never lost sight of her dream man. When the band began playing a Sam Cooke classic and Dexter began walking toward her, Faye's heart almost dropped to her toes. *He can't be coming over here.* She looked behind her. That table was empty, its occupants already on the dance floor. *No! Not me! He can't possibly think I'd—*

"Dance? Please?"

That smile is deadly. Lethal. Should require a permit and be concealed in public. "No, thank you. I don't dance."

"Nonsense." He grabbed her hand before she could move it, began gently pulling her up. It felt as though all eyes were on her, her tablemates smiling and prodding her on. There was no way she could resist without looking silly. "I've got you," he whispered as he pulled her up against him. She hung on—not because she was trying to make a romantic move, but because she really couldn't dance! Especially the way he was turning and rocking back and forth. Fortunately for both of them he was an excellent leader, and she was more than content to follow where he led her. The song spoke of thrills and kisses, infatuation and longing, and sending people places, and with Faye feeling Dexter's arms around her and smelling the musky manliness of his cologne, her head was spinning with the desire to experience them all with him!

The song ended and still she clung to him. It had been the most thrilling three minutes she'd experienced in a long time. She didn't want to let go. "That was amazing." *Oops. Wait. Did I say that out loud?*

"You are amazing."

Yes, girl, those words actually came out of your mouth.

"My turn!" A fiery redhead came to steal away Dexter, and the spell was broken. Faye went back to her seat, and after awhile sanity joined her there. But not before reliving how those arms felt around her and how that chest felt up against hers, oh, about a hundred millions times. By the time the band was reminding the revelers that it didn't mean a thing if it didn't have that swing, Faye was back out on the dance floor, this time with the businessman from Texas. The day had turned out to be fun after all.

On the other side of the garden, Dexter joined his sister, Diamond, and their older brother, Donovan. They all watched their great-grandfather enjoy his moment in the sun.

"Ooh, look at Birdie," Diamond said, giving a surreptitious nod to the scowling woman sitting at the table Papa Dee had occupied. "She does not appreciate Charlotte dancing with her man!"

"They both better watch out for Kat," Donovan chimed, as he watched Diamond's assistant, a Drake employee for over twenty years, make a beeline for where Papa Dee was dancing. "I think she's getting ready to cut in!"

Sure enough the plucky, red-headed Irishwoman kindly took Papa Dee's hand, placed an arm around his back and joined him in his rock around the clock. A semicircle formed around them as they danced, the audience clapping and cheering them on. The song ended. Papa Dee bowed.

"Such a gentleman," Diamond cooed, putting a hand on her round belly.

"What a man," Dexter agreed.

They all watched as the patriarch who'd lived to see five generations took one step, and then another and then fell over.

Chapter 8

Mayhem ensued.

The Drake clan surged toward their fallen patriarch, with Dexter leading the charge. "Move back!" he demanded. Reaching the man he'd idolized since before he knew the word's meaning, he bent down to scoop him up. Just as he prepared to lift him, a voice even more commanding than his had been cut through the din of chaos.

"Do not move him!"

As one, the crowd turned toward the source of the sound. Faye moved quickly and decisively, her actions coming by rote. She'd weathered warfare in Africa, hurricane threats in Haiti. Her movements were automatic. All thoughts save those of the man on the ground—including the handsome man hovering over him—fled from her mind.

"Please. Let me through. I'm a doctor." She dropped to her knees and placed two fingers under Papa Dee's nose.

He was not breathing. "Call 911." Her voice was calm, authoritative, almost soothing in its surety. "Everyone step back. He needs air." Everyone moved except Dexter, who stayed as if glued to his great-grandfather's side. She loosened Papa Dee's tie, ripped apart his shirt and spoke methodically. "I'm going to administer CPR." She opened Papa Dee's airway by tilting back his head. When still not detecting a breath, she covered his mouth with hers and sent two quick bursts of air into his body, followed by thirty chest compressions delivered between the ribcage and chest. Considering his age, she was careful to keep her hands directly over his sternum. Even so, she knew the chances were great that a rib would get broken. To save his life, however, it was a chance she had to take. The process was repeated. Breathe into the body. Chest compressions. Check for breath. Again. Finally, Papa Dee moaned. Very slight. Almost inaudible. But it was a sound.

Fortunately, not the only one. The blare of sirens could be heard in the distance. Faye looked up and caught Dexter's panicked eyes boring into hers. "Someone needs to direct the paramedics to where we are."

As if a sprinter's gun had been fired, Dexter was up and moving through the crowd. The resort's security team worked to keep the guests at bay although honestly, respect for the man they'd come to celebrate kept most everyone at a respectable distance.

Within seconds, paramedics stormed in. As one kneeled down to begin work on Papa Dee, Faye addressed another one. "I'm Dr. Buckner. It seems we have a man with a heart condition. The patient has been somewhat stabilized, but we need to get him quickly to the hospital."

They secured an oxygen mask on Papa Dee, put him on a stretcher and quickly wheeled him around to the side entrance. Dexter walked briskly alongside the gurney. The paramedic to whom Faye had been speaking uttered a quick "thanks" before turning to run behind the other.

She stayed him with a hand on his arm. "What hospital?"

"Loma Linda." And then he was gone.

Faye turned and went in the opposite direction, away from the side entrance and toward the front entrance, which was closest to the hotel and its parking lot. Only one thing was on her mind: getting her credentials and then locating the hospital through her GPS. Thankfully, she'd had only one flute of champagne, had taken only one sip from the second that had been offered during the toast. In the space of a few minutes, Papa Dee had gone from being a person whose party she was attending to a person whose life had been in her hands. As a doctor who practiced with her heart, she had to make sure her patient was all right. She wouldn't be able to rest until she knew.

Within the span of fifteen minutes, Faye was taking the Clinton-Keith exit off I-215. After two more left turns she arrived at the hospital, parked in a designated spot and entered through the emergency entrance.

"Hello," she said to the receptionist at the desk. "I'm Dr. Buckner, and I'm here to check on a patient, David Drake Sr. He came in probably five, ten minutes ago suffering from cardiac arrest and perhaps other complications." She placed her credentials down on the desk as she spoke.

"Yes, Doctor," the receptionist replied after a quick perusal of Faye's ID, the keys on her computer being clicked rapidly as she viewed the screen. "He's in emergency right now."

"The attending physician?"

More key clicks. "Dr. Saunders. I'm not sure we can get you into the emergency room—"

"That won't be necessary. I can speak with the doctor when he's finished. Which way to the waiting room?"

"Right around the corner. You can't miss it."

"Thank you." Faye rounded the corner. Dexter was the first sight she saw.

She stopped.

He stopped. His eyes were glassy; worry was painted all over his face. "You're a doctor."

"Yes, I am."

"My great-grandfather. Do you think…"

"We don't know, Dexter. But he was breathing when the paramedics arrived and his heartbeat, while not overly strong, was steady. His skin tone looked good, and there was no drastic drop in his body temperature. I think the best thing for him right now is all of us thinking positive thoughts and believing in the best possible outcome."

"You're right." He continued looking at her. His expression was unreadable. "Thank you."

As he looked into her doe-brown eyes and she stared into his brownish-hazel orbs, something happened. A heat, low and mostly unidentifiable, passed between them. The same as the one she'd felt on the dance floor while in his arms. Then, like now, it was gone in an instant.

"I was headed to the waiting room." Faye walked past him and into the room, where various families huddled with combinations of faith and worry, hope and fear. Her targeted destination was easy to spot. Decked out in their party wear, the Drake clan, along with concerned employees who'd come in on their day off to recognize the founder, took up a third of the room. Halfway there, the man she remembered as the son of Papa Dee spotted her. He said something to the group and a dozen heads swiveled in her direction.

"Doctor." David Drake Jr. was the first to speak.

"How is he?"

"What happened?"

"Is he going to be all right?"

These questions rang out at once. Faye raised her hands to still them. "I just now arrived and haven't been in the emergency room or spoken to the attending physician. The nurse says he's stable, and when she has a moment, she'll let the team know I'm here."

"What do you think happened to my father?" David Jr.'s voice was strong, but deep concern shown in his eyes.

Faye was almost sure that Papa Dee had suffered a heart attack, but she wasn't certain so she wouldn't share. "It's best not to speculate," she said instead, her voice automatically calm and soothing from years of comforting the afflicted. "In times like these it's difficult, but if you'll try to remain calm and keep your thoughts positive, that's often the best for your loved one."

"The doctor's right," Dexter added. He placed a hand on Faye's shoulder. Only now did she realize he'd been standing just behind her; only now was she aware of the source of the woodsy scent that had tickled her nostrils. "Y'all know how Papa is. He wouldn't want us out here crying and carrying on." Dexter said the words in the raspy voice of his great-grandfather. "Or getting our faces twisted up." Another Papa Deeism.

A kind-looking older woman approached Faye. "Hello, I'm Mary Drake, David Jr.'s wife. We're so thankful that you were there today. Are you a resident of Temecula?"

"No, ma'am. I'm a guest at the hotel."

This news elicited a variety of facial expressions: surprise, delight, curiosity.

"Donald Drake here," a tall, imposing man announced, coming forward with hand outstretched. "I'm David Sr.'s grandson and the president of the hotel. What is your name, Doctor?"

"Faye Buckner."

"How long have you been at our establishment?"

"Just arrived yesterday. I'll be staying for a week."

"Well, on behalf of myself, my wife—". he gestured toward an attractive, slim woman whose expression suggested that her thoughts were in overdrive "—and the entire Drake family, let us thank you for stepping in today and helping our patriarch by considering you our guest during your stay."

Faye's brow furrowed. She was already a guest at the hotel. How else would she consider herself? "Thank you," she said, hoping it was an appropriate response to what she thought an obvious statement.

The woman who'd been introduced as Donald's wife stepped forward. "Dear, would you like to sit down? It may be a while before the doctor comes out."

Faye nodded and followed the elegance-oozing woman to a row of chairs. On the way, she caught a look pass between Dexter and his sister, and saw a wisp of a smile cut through the worry lines.

"I'm Genevieve Drake," the woman said as soon as they were seated. "David Jr. and Mary are my husband's parents—my in-laws." She nodded toward the three people still standing. "Those are our children. Donovan, he's the oldest. Diamond is my only daughter and Dexter our youngest son."

"You have a beautiful family," Faye said sincerely.

"Thank you. We're very blessed."

"Yes. You are."

"What about you? Are you here visiting with your husband?"

"No, Mrs. Drake. I'm not married."

A perfectly arched brow rose ever so slightly. "Oh?"

"No, ma'am, I'm single."

"Single as in never married?"

"Correct."

"Do you have children? I don't mean to pry, but you're smart, attractive…I'm curious."

Faye chased away the discomfort that usually came with this topic of conversation. At thirty-two years old, it was one she'd had often. "I understand. No, I don't have any—"

"Excuse me, ladies," Dexter interrupted. "Faye, you have the distinct look of one being interrogated. Is my mother asking for your date of birth and Social Security number?"

"We're just talking," Faye said with a smile, hiding the sigh of relief that she'd been rescued.

"Yes, I'm very familiar with how my mother loves to talk," he said with a smirk. "All of that listening has probably made you thirsty. Would you like to join me in a hunt for the cafeteria or somewhere to get bottled water?"

Faye stood. "Sure."

They turned to leave, just in time to see the doctor entering the waiting room and walking toward them. The men were on their feet in an instant.

"How is he, Doc?" Donald asked.

The others gathered around the doctor. "He's weak, but he's going to be okay." The expression on the Drakes' faces was a collective one of relief. Faye could have sworn that a little more air seeped into the room. "Where is Dr. Buckner?" The doctor looked around the group.

Faye stepped forward. "Right here," she said, hand outstretched. "You must be Dr. Saunders."

"Yes. I understand that you attended the patient until paramedics arrived?"

"Yes."

"Good work. Thanks to your quick actions, there appears to be no permanent damage to any major organs, including the heart."

David Jr., who was just an inch shorter than his six-foot son, Donald, came to stand beside him. "What happened, Doctor?"

"And you are?"

"I'm the patient's son."

The doctor nodded and shook the outstretched hand. "Mr. Drake suffered what's known as a coronary artery spasm—in layman's terms, a very mild heart attack."

"Oh, goodness!" Mary cried, voicing what some of the others had felt. Her own father had died when she was thirty, just ten years after she and David Jr. had married. Now, at seventy-eight, she'd known Papa Dee longer than she'd known her own flesh and blood, and loved him not one bit less. "A heart attack is serious. What are you going to do? A bypass? How can you say that he'll be fine?"

"Your concern is understandable," Dr. Saunders replied, his voice firm and matter-of-fact. "Heart attacks can be very serious, and very damaging. Fortunately, what Mr. Drake experienced is the very least of what can happen when the artery wall tightens and blood flow through that artery is restricted."

"What is the treatment?" Dexter appeared calmer than he'd looked since Papa Dee dropped to the ground.

"We're still performing tests to determine plaque buildup and other potential causes for the blockage, but in most cases the problems can be solved with medication."

"Can we see him?"

"He's still in ICU, but we'll have him in a private room shortly. The nurse will let you know when he's been moved."

The family asked a few more questions, received the

doctor's reassurances and then sat down to wait. Only after looking around the room and then the hallways did Dexter realize that sometime during Dr. Saunders' explanation, the angel who'd likely saved his great-grandfather's life had left Loma Linda.

Chapter 9

At midnight the previous evening, after being reassured by the hospital staff that his great-grandfather would sleep through the night, Dexter had gone home. Now, at 5:30 a.m., he was headed back to Loma Linda. When Papa Dee opened his eyes, Dexter wanted to be there.

As he drove, listening to the sounds of Nat King Cole, another of Papa Dee's favorites, he thought of Faye Buckner. She wasn't his type, given; definitely not like anyone he'd ever dated before. *A study in contradictions.* Yes, that was it. Like the bare-faced woman wearing the faded jeans and wrinkled tee compared with the sexy chick who'd shown up at the party in dress and heels with a smart new hairdo that highlighted her high cheekbones and wide, bright eyes. Like the tentative, shy personality who'd barely said three words when he'd first approached her before the party to the self-assured take-charge doctor—*doctor!*—who'd commanded that he leave his great-grandfather where he lay.

"Who are you really?" he muttered, pulling into the hospital parking lot and bounding out of his sports car seconds after the wheels had stopped rolling. He entered the lobby and strolled to the front desk, unmindful of the subtle and not so subtle looks by every female in the room. "I'm here to see David Drake Sr.," he said, blessing the receptionist with a smile as bright as the early morning sun.

"And you are?" the woman asked, and actually tried to act as though the question had been asked for professional reasons.

Dexter leaned on the counter. "My name is Dexter Drake," he said, with a quick glance at her name badge. "Do you have any other questions for me, Veronica? Or will you just be a darling and tell me where I can find my relative?"

"Of course, Dexter," the pretty blonde replied. "Here, let me write down his room number." She did, adding another ten numbers beneath it, along with her name. "Have a good day!" she sang to his retreating back.

Dexter turned the corner, nodded at a couple of ogling nurses and reached the room number written on the slip of paper. Taking a deep breath, he slowly opened the door. The sight that greeted him caused him to stagger against the wall, close his eyes and will down his emotions. Papa Dee looked pale and ashen. Against the stark white of the sheets and hospital gown, his frame seemed smaller, thinner than just the day before. In other words, for the first time in Dexter's memory, his great-grandfather looked closer to his actual age. For the first time in about fifteen years, since the time Papa Dee fell off a horse, Dexter briefly entertained the thought of life without one of his best friends. He couldn't. Not now.

After several long minutes, Dexter pried himself from the wall and walked over to the bed. He looked at the screen of the device hooked up to Papa Dee, showing squiggles and numbers and letters like BPM and NBP. On the other side of the bed was a pole holding a bag of fluid, a tube traveling from there to Papa Dee's hand, where the needle allowing delivery of those fluids into his great-grandfather's body was taped in place. Dexter took his large, strong index finger and outlined the veins on Papa Dee's hand. *Have they always been this pronounced?* He gave a light squeeze, looked into his great-grandfather's face and felt his heart constrict. "Hang in there, old man," he said aloud. "This is no way to get out of a chess match. I'm still going to whoop that ass."

Lashes fluttered. Lips pursed. An eye worked to open.

"I thought that might get you," Dexter said, with a smile in his voice. "All of this just so you wouldn't have to dance with Birdie." *Ah, yes. A wisp of a smile.* "Just relax, Papa. Don't let me bother you. I'll just take a seat by the window until you wake up."

A soft sound escaped Papa Dee's mouth. He cleared his throat as his eyes fluttered open. "Where…am…I?" His voice was barely above a whisper.

"You're at the hospital, Papa. Remember, we told you last night, when you woke up."

Papa Dee tried to look around, but moving his head from side to side was too much work. "Hospital?"

"Shh, come on, now, Pops. Don't worry about it. Just lie there and get your rest. The doctor will be here in a minute to explain everything. Mama and Daddy will be here soon, and the grands are on their way, too."

"Woman?" Papa Dee whispered, his eyes closing.

"What did you say, Papa?" He didn't answer. "Are you thirsty? Do you want some water?"

"Woman," Papa Dee repeated with a slight shake of his head.

"Are you already eyeing the pretty nurses? Here you are flat on your back and still trying to be a player. You're something else, Papa. You just stay relaxed. I'm going to go and find the doctor."

Back at Drake Resort, Faye rolled over and enjoyed a good stretch. She looked at the clock and was surprised to see that it was just 7 a.m. Given that she'd gone to bed at eleven the night before, however, she felt rested. And restless. This vacation stuff was not for the faint of heart. And yesterday's events had nudged the doctor within her, made her miss Haiti and practicing medicine, and all the friends and stalwart natives of that country she'd left behind.

When Faye had arrived in Port-au-Prince just after the worse earthquake to hit that area in almost a century, it was to sheer devastation. Hospitals had been totally destroyed along with most other buildings. Death and injuries were everywhere. She'd deplaned, checked in with the Red Cross and worked a solid seventy-two hours without sleep. More crew arrived and the pace slightly lessened. But the sick and injured remained, keeping the doctors who'd flown in busy for the next six months. During this time she met Adeline, the daughter of a Haitian diplomat who'd died in the quake. Adeline had poured her grief into the founding of Haitian Heartbeats, and soon Dr. Ian Chapollow heard of her efforts and became a board member and resident doctor. He'd hired Faye and the rest was history. Faye became not only his protégé but the daughter he never had. He became a father figure, providing acknowledgment and encouragement that had been sorely lacking in her life since her own father's death so many years ago. For the first time since those late night chats with Ger-

ald McPherson, Faye had shared with someone her hopes
and dreams of one day returning to the United States and
helping the underprivileged. As the years passed more
medical help arrived, and the stream of patients lessened.
Dr. Ian convinced her that now was the time to make her
move. If not for the prodding of Dr. Ian, Faye would still
be in Haiti, sharing a modest duplex with a nurse and a
rescued yellow Lab named Lucy, driving a beat-up Jeep,
and loving every minute of it.

After checking emails and then luxuriating in the wide
marble shower with its multiple heads and floating bench,
Faye dressed in workout gear and prepared to leave the
room. "Let's see…room card, cell phone. Do I need my
cell phone?" A knock interrupted her internal debate. She
looked at the clock. *Who's at my door at eight o'clock in
the morning?* She looked out the peephole and was surprised to see a hotel worker holding a large basket with a
big red bow.

"Good morning, ma'am!" The worker's blue eyes spar-
kled as he held the large basket. "Delivery for Dr. Faye
Buckner. May I put this on the table?"

"For me?"

"Absolutely." The hotel employee beamed.

"Are you sure?" She'd spoken to her family and told
them where she was staying but doubted her mother or
brother would send such a gift. They'd never before presented her with "welcome home" flowers and her birthday was still four months away. Still, she moved aside so
that the young man could enter.

"Enjoy!" He turned to leave.

"Wait—let me get your tip." Faye walked toward where
her purse sat in a chair next to the window.

"No need, ma'am. You are the resort's special guest.

This is my pleasure." Before Faye could get over her shock and formulate a sentence, he was gone.

Special guest? Faye walked over to the basket and took the card out of the envelope pinned to the bow.

Dr. Buckner:

Thank you for your quick actions yesterday. We are sure that it helped our loved one survive. On behalf of the Drake family and this resort, please accept this basket and complimentary use of our entire facility including restaurant, wine bar, spa, salon and hotel gift shop during your stay. The cost of the room has been credited back to the card from which it was debited...with our deepest and most sincere gratitude.

The Drakes

"What?" Faye looked around as if somehow the empty room would give her an answer, and then back to the lovely arrangement. For a second she wondered if Dexter had orchestrated the floral delivery and immediately warmed at the thought. Then she remembered Donald and his comment. *Let us thank you for stepping in today and helping our patriarch by considering you our guest during your stay.* Now it made sense. She was now staying at this luxurious, five-star resort for free, and being encouraged to take advantage of its upscale amenities! *For simply being who I am and doing my job?* Faye was impressed at the generous offer, but it was too much. She couldn't do anything about the room cost since she hadn't purchased it in the first place. But she had every intention of paying for any services she received.

Her first test came in the Grapevine, the hotel's comfortably appointed restaurant. After a delightful breakfast of fresh fruit, a bagel and two scrambled eggs, she requested the bill.

"Would you like the total added to your room bill?" the waiter asked.

"No, I'd like to pay now, please." She pulled out a credit card and handed it to the waiter.

After a few minutes, the waiter returned. "I'm so sorry, Dr. Buckner. I didn't realize it was you. Please accept the breakfast with our compliments."

"Thank you, but I'd really like to pay."

The waiter's eyes widened in alarm, his head shook slowly. "Oh, no. We cannot accept your card." He lowered his voice. "My job would be on the line, and we couldn't have that, now could we?" Wink.

"No," Faye said, determined to be gracious until she could speak to one of the Drakes. "The meal was delicious. Thank you."

Faye worked out for an hour, came back up to the room for another quick shower, and then hit the road in her rented Hyundai. She went to an area of Temecula called Old Town, three quaint blocks filled with boutiques, restaurants and tourists. On the corner was a small building touting a sign: Tarot/Palm Readings. Faye immediately thought of Dexter. *Don't need a psychic to tell me what I already know.* He'd been gracious and attentive at the hospital but she deduced that that was less about a personal interest in her and more about deep concern for his great-grandfather. *He's probably already forgotten about me.* The woman who ended up with Dexter Drake would more than likely look as though she stepped off the pages of *Glamour* magazine. She thought about Diamond, still gorgeous in the last few months of pregnancy, and the dark-skinned woman with the long, thick hair and curvy figure; the one who she now guessed was Dexter's brother's wife. Both women dripped culture, sophistication, that city-girl vibe that Faye could never imagine having.

She spent an hour meandering through the shops in Old Town and then decided to go back to the Promenade Mall, where she'd shopped the day before and had also noticed a movie theater. After enjoying her first movie on the big screen in almost two years, she returned to the resort, ready to get in a few hours of work before deciding on what she wanted for dinner. She'd just fired up her computer when the hotel phone rang.

"Hello?"

"Dr. Buckner?"

That voice. Those chills. The tingle. "Yes?"

"It's Dexter."

Breathe, Faye. It's a necessary component to living. "How's your great-grandfather?"

"He's coming around. He asked about you."

"Really? I'm surprised he remembered me." *I am even more shocked that you're calling me!* "He was barely conscious when they took him away."

"You don't know Papa. He never forgets a pretty face. They're going to keep him a few days for observation, get him rehydrated, but after that we should have him back as good as new."

"That's good news." Faye hoped that was the right answer because honestly, she hadn't heard much past the pretty face remark.

"My family can't thank you enough."

"Yes, you can. And you have. In fact, I need to speak with you about my being your special guest. I can't possibly—"

"Join me for dinner tonight?"

"Excuse me?"

"Meet me in the lobby. Say, seven-thirty?"

"There's no need to feel obligated to take me out."

"Good…because I don't. Now, put on something sexy

like what you wore at the party. And wear that lipstick that you had on earlier, too. That pink shade looked nice on you."

Five minutes later and Faye was still thinking about Dexter's lipstick comment. Did men actually pay attention to such things? Obviously they did. Which meant one thing: he'd been really checking her out while they were dancing. Looking at her lips! She only hoped he hadn't seen her lick them while she'd looked at him.

Chapter 10

Put on something sexy. The exact advice and the exact words her friend Addie had used two days before. Faye huffed as she fingered the meager collection that served as her new wardrobe. Her clothing collection wasn't extensive by any means, and the bulk of it was being shipped with her other personal items that were due to arrive next week. Focusing her thoughts on the closet once again, she went from the "little black dress" that she'd worn in Haiti for the past two years to the turquoise-blue, knee-length number that due to the clerk's insistence she'd purchased on Friday. "That color looks so good on you," the woman had insisted. Holding it up to herself as she looked into the floor-length mirror, she had to agree that the color did do wonderful things against her skin tone. *But is it too dressy? Will it look as though I'm trying to impress?* "Aren't you trying to impress?" asked the imp on her shoulder.

"No," was her less-than-truthful verbal reply.

She put on the dress along with the sparkly heels she'd worn to the party. And in spite of her rational claims to the contrary, she felt just a little like Cinderella.

At 7:28, Faye walked out of the elevators into the bustling lobby of the Drake Hotel. She could hear music oozing out of the Vineyard, the property's lounge/nightclub, and watched as women in five-inch heels and men in suit jackets headed toward the establishment's doors. Interestingly enough, there seemed nothing incongruous about the women in flats and the men in shorts who also trickled inside.

At 7:30 exactly, Dexter walked through the hotel's revolving doors. Faye turned as he entered and willed herself not to react to six feet two inches of mesmerizing manliness; tried not to notice how the casual navy blue summer suit fit his lean frame to perfection. Or how the stark white shirt highlighted his bronzed skin. Or how the tailored jacket emphasized strong, broad shoulders. Or how he brought about feelings similar to the ones she'd felt in her dream.

"Good evening, Doctor," Dexter said when he reached her, giving her body a quick sweep that caused chill bumps and heat surges at the same time.

"Good evening, Dexter."

"You look good."

"Darn," she replied, her face in a mock pout. "I was going for sexy."

His eyes darkened. Seconds passed before he spoke. "That, too." Faye wanted to take the lips through which those words had been uttered and press them against her own. Fortunately, before she could act on such a rash impulse, he held out his arm. "Shall we?"

After a slight hesitation, Faye linked her arm with his. She was more than a little aware of the stares their exit elicited, sure that the women were wondering how she'd gotten so lucky. It wasn't that Faye was insecure. She was a realist aware of her shortcomings in the looks department. How many times as a child had she been teased because her nose was too wide, and as a teen that her breasts were too small? There was one particular nemesis who harassed her almost every day of her existence during her junior high school days. "Frank, oops, I mean Faye," he'd say with his ever-present posse in tow. "Thought you were a dude." The crowd would laugh at him as though he were a shoo-in for Saturday Night Live.

"You're lame and lackadaisical," she'd retort, leaving him to wonder about her five-syllable put-down. Last she heard he'd fallen on hard times and was sweeping the floors of that same school. Karma was a bitch.

They arrived at a shiny, sleek black sports car. He opened her car door and once she was safely inside, bounded around to the driver's side and let himself in.

"Been in one of these before?" he asked somewhat smugly, as he put the Maserati GranCabrio into reverse and eased out of the parking space.

"A two-door?" Faye quipped with feigned innocence, buckling her belt. "Sure. My first car was a Honda Civic two-door with bucket seats. Very similar to this."

"Ha-ha, very funny," Dexter said, though inwardly he was a tad bit offended that she'd compare his luxury vehicle to a bucket on wheels. He tapped the gas and the car soared forward. Its power was undeniable yet inside you could barely hear the engine.

"Okay, admittedly it wasn't this sporty. But it got me everywhere I wanted to go."

"And where was that?"

"Back in the mid-nineties?" She shrugged. "School, work, the library, home. That's about it."

"Where are you from?"

Dexter shifted gears and accidentally brushed Faye's leg in the process. Faye unconsciously shifted said leg closer, hoping that he'd brush it again.

"I was born in North Carolina but grew up mainly in Saint Louis. My dad was in the army. We moved around a lot until I was eleven years old."

"And then he retired?"

A pause and then, "He died."

"I'm sorry." The sincerity in his voice was palpable. "That must have been hard."

"It was. My mom remarried and we moved to the Midwest. I lived there until I went off to college."

"Where'd you study?"

"Johns Hopkins."

Dexter whistled. "Nice."

"What about you?"

"Cornell." Faye reacted before she could hide her surprise. "Didn't see that one coming, did you?"

"I'm sorry. It's just that…"

"You thought I was a spoiled trust-fund brother who hadn't had to earn my position at Drake Wines. I came into a blessed family, but we believe in hard work. None of us were given our positions. We trained and competed for them. My undergrad is in viticulture and enology. My grad is in business." Dexter gave her a crooked smile. "You can be duly impressed."

"You're doing that on purpose."

"What?"

"Acting conceited."

"Maybe."

Faye noted that they'd gotten on the I-15 freeway, heading south. She also noticed the melodic sounds playing softly from the stereo system. "Nice music."

"You like?" Dexter turned it up a bit. "It's a band I'm backing called Seven Day Weekend. The lead guitarist is a childhood friend of mine."

Faye nodded. "Did you grow up on the resort?"

"I grew up on the vineyard. It didn't become a resort until a couple years ago." He told her about the expansion project that had been largely headed by his father, Donald, his brother, Donovan, and his sister, Diamond.

"It must be nice to have such a close-knit family." She turned to him. "At least, that's how it appears."

"In this instance, looks are not deceiving. We all dearly love each other…and like each other most of the time."

Faye laughed. The sound warmed Dexter's heart.

"I can tell. Yesterday just watching how you guys interacted, the love was evident."

"Ah. So you've been checking me out."

Arrogant much? Still, Faye blushed. It was true. She'd taken every opportunity that he was in her line of sight to drink in his fineness. But he didn't need to know that. "I've been observing my surroundings."

"Ha!" For Faye, Dexter's knowing chuckle warmed several places. "Do you have siblings?"

"A brother, Richard, from my mom's second marriage. We're ten years apart and not so close. I was gone and in college by the time he was eight. Then I joined the Peace Corps, spent five years in Africa and left there to go to Haiti and help the earthquake victims. In between, I only went back home a handful of times."

"What made you want to be a doctor?"

Faye looked out the window and into yesterday. Her smile was bittersweet as she spoke. "I was seven years old. My dad and I were walking in a park and came upon a young bird with a broken wing. It was lying there, a weak chirp coming out every few seconds. I was distraught and refused to walk away and leave it there. My dad found a piece of cardboard, and we made a nest of grass and leaves and took it home. There, we transferred the nest to a shoebox. My dad made a splint with Popsicle sticks and secured the wing to the bird's body with a strip of gauze. I went to the library to find out what they ate, and I fed it worms, watered-down cat food and water from a dropper. One day about three weeks later we took off the gauze and splint and the wing had healed! It was like a miracle that something had been broken and I had fixed it," Faye continued, her voice soft, reflective. "I went to school that day happy and skipping and giving everyone the good news. When I returned to see Robin after school—" her smile faded"—she'd flown away."

"What kind of bird was it?"

Faye looked at Dexter, brows creased. "A robin. Why?"

"Curious."

"Your care seems genuine. I wouldn't have guessed it."

"You're nothing if not straightforward. Many women aren't." They'd reached their destination. Dexter pulled up to the valet. "You're different."

"Is that why you asked me out? Because I'm different from the beautiful, sophisticated women you usually date?"

Dexter gave her a look that jiggled her insides. "Don't underestimate yourself, Doctor."

Faye became silent, content to listen to the sounds of smooth jazz. She didn't know what to make of Dexter Drake. She did know that she wanted to make out with him. This realization, on top of everything else that had happened since she'd arrived in California, had her flustered.

They reached the door and were quickly seated as soon

as they entered the restaurant. "Mexican food is my favorite. Haven't had it in awhile."

"This is some of the best in San Diego," Dexter offered. "It's Mexican with a twist." Faye raised a brow. "Mexican-French," he explained. "Prepare to be amazed."

The chef came out and greeted Dexter by name. They chatted for a few moments before he turned to Faye. "Would you allow me the pleasure of ordering for you?"

"Sure."

Soon after he'd placed their order, the waiter brought over a bottle of wine.

"Compliments of the chef," he said, before opening it and pouring out a small amount for Dexter to sample.

He did so. "Not bad for Napa," he said with a smirk.

The waiter shrugged. "What can I say, Mr. Drake?"

"It's fine."

The waiter poured their drinks and left. Dexter raised his glass.

"Do you mind if I stick to my lemon water? I'm not much of a drinker."

"Suit yourself. To what should we toast?"

"To the totally restored health of your great-grandfather?" Faye asked, hoisting her glass.

"That," Dexter said, giving Faye a look that was part devil, part dare, "and injured birds learning to fly."

It was not the toast she expected. He wasn't the man she expected. This wasn't the night she expected. But rather than let a myriad of thoughts overtake her, or fears defy her, she simply replied, "Cheers."

Chapter 11

Over mushrooms marinated in lime juice, olive oil, onions, tomatoes, cilantro and serrano chillies, and Mexican tapas, Faye learned that Dexter had been labeled a gifted child by his elementary teachers, had excelled in sports and grades in middle school, and was the sports star, ladies' man and president of his senior high school class.

During the main course, *huachinango al queso y chipotle* for Faye and *medallion de camarones al chile guajillo* for Dexter, Dexter explained how he'd wowed everyone on his college campus with brawn, brains and dancing skill; how he'd been recruited to run track and had almost turned pro; and had helped lead his junior track team to a regional first-place finish. She savored her fresh red snapper with chipotle cream and Oaxaca cheese. He devoured large shrimp wrapped in bacon, served with Oaxaca cheese gratin and a light *guajillo* sauce. He talked about his years of dodging determined females and leaving broken hearts from Ithaca, NY, to wine country, CA. She laughed. And listened, hearing more of the Dexter that she'd previously expected. Cool. Confident. Charismatic.

The waiter removed their entrée plates. Dexter sat back, obviously satisfied with the meal. "How are you enjoying the meal so far?"

"Absolutely delicious," Faye said, wiping her mouth with a napkin. "Some of the best food I've ever eaten."

"Do you have room for dessert?"

"Do you?" Dexter gave her a quizzical look. "I mean, after all, you seem so full of yourself."

"Whoa!"

A smile softened Faye's carefully delivered jab.

"That's really how you feel about me? After I've spent the evening baring my soul, letting you know all my secrets?"

"Baring your soul? I think that's a stretch."

"It is. But I don't know," Dexter continued, eyeing Faye speculatively. "There's something about you that makes me feel like I can tell you anything. I don't know if that's a good thing."

"I don't either."

"Ha!"

The two shared Mexican flan and then left the restaurant stuffed and satisfied.

"I'm going to sleep good tonight," Faye said, once they'd settled into the buttery leather seats of Dexter's ride.

"Thinking about bed, are we?" Faye rolled her eyes. "So tell me, Doctor. Does your battling wars and quakes and saving lives leave any time for love?"

"Not really." She tried to answer the question as casually as it had been asked.

"Is that by choice?"

No! A part of Faye had always wanted to be a wife and

mother, a superwoman able to juggle kiddies and career and leap tall buildings with a single bound. But early rejections in those formative years had built in a defense mechanism that had left her guarded, wary and slow to trust. Her father's death had taught her that loving unconditionally and absolutely could be painful, and that the love of your life could leave you without a moment's notice or a backward glance.

"C'mon, now," Dexter kidded. "Tell me about all those peers and patients you've strung along those hospital corridors."

You mean all two of them? "Unlike you, Dexter Drake, I am not a player…or a flirt."

"I've been known for being both of them," Dexter admitted. "I'm not going to lie about that."

"He's nothing if not honest," Faye mumbled to the passing mountains, mimicking what Dexter had earlier said.

"The thing about me," Dexter continued, "is that I'm clear about who I am, what I want and how I act in relationships. I talk straight, am upfront, and no woman has to guess what's going on between us."

"And that justifies your lifestyle?"

"Are you judging my lifestyle?"

"No. You just remind me of a boy I've hated since my teenage years."

"Damn."

"No," Faye hurried to correct. "I don't hate you. That statement wasn't about you. It was about me, and the insecurities born in my childhood and teenaged years. Larry Chambers was in my eighth-grade class. He looked like a teenaged Will Smith and everyone loved him. When it came to popularity he could make you or break you, and I was his comedy relief. He called me Frank or Olive Oil from Popeye, depending on the day. I was already intro-

verted and this type of attention was excruciating. Sorry...
I just had a flashback moment. I guess being back in the
States will do that to you." Faye was embarrassed, but felt
strangely liberated, as well. She was no longer close to
hyperventilating when being in His Highness's presence.
He felt more like a brother now, or one of the boys in the
operating room. "Now you're becoming the person I feel
I can tell everything, too."

"Ah, Doctor, are we going to become pals?"

Faye slid him a glance. "Maybe."

Small talk punctuated long moments of companionable
silence as they made the forty-five-minute trip from outer
San Diego back to the resort. Dexter pulled into a reserved
parking spot at the front of the hotel, cut the engine and
then walked around to open the door for Faye.

She smiled, shyly, guiltily, as though the bubble that had
surrounded them in his luxury car and the restaurant had
burst; the golden carriage had turned back into a pumpkin
and her glass slipper was simply a Bebe slingback after all.

"Thanks for dinner," she said as soon as she'd exited
his vehicle, eager to be alone and in her room so that she
could assess the night.

"The night is young," Dexter replied and much to Faye's
chagrin fell in step beside her and accompanied her into
the hotel. "Would you like to check out the lounge, or take
a turn on the dance floor? The lounge is more laid-back.
The club will let us get our party on."

They'd reached the middle of the lobby; still fairly
crowded. It was Saturday night, after all. "Thanks but I
think I'll pass. I think the nonstop pace of the past few
years is catching up with me. A pillow is calling my name."

"All right then," Dexter replied, once again placing a
gentle hand on her elbow and steering them toward the
elevators. "Let's get you tucked in."

"Oh, no, that won't be necessary." The look on Faye's face made it clear that "tucking" was not exactly what she thought he had on his mind!

"My bad." Dexter pushed the elevator button, his attitude nonplussed. "Figure of speech. But I will be a gentleman and see you to your door."

The elevator came. They entered. The ride to Faye's floor and the walk to the door of her suite were quiet.

"Thanks again," Faye said, fumbling for her key card. "It was a very nice evening."

"My pleasure," Dexter said, his voice slightly husky as he gently removed the card from Faye's hand. He kept his gaze locked with hers as he unlocked her door. He took a step, one that put his body within inches of hers; so close that she could feel his heat, imagine his "intention."

"Okay, so, goodnight." She averted her eyes and held out her hand. *Please! Just give me my key card before I die!*

But, no. That would have been too much like right. He had to place one hand on her shoulder and another on her chin, had to turn her head ever so slightly. Had to run his hand down her arm as he bent down his head and placed a kiss—soft and feathery—on her parted lips.

"Good night, Doctor," he murmured.

"Good night." She walked into the room, turned and offered as best a smile as she could muster under the circumstances (keeping her knees from buckling and her heart from beating out her chest) and closed the door.

Inside the room, silence enveloped her. That…and abject loneliness unlike she'd ever felt. She leaned against the door, took several calming breaths and asked herself the million-dollar question: *What. Just. Happened?*

Chapter 12

The next day, Dexter found himself asking a similar question. He'd think about Faye at the oddest times: while coming from the east wing where he resided to join his parents in the dining room, when mixing various types of grapes for the company's latest wine offering and last night, while hanging with some of his friends in the local casino's high-limits room. That had surprised him. Normally nothing came between him and his rare games of poker. He thought of her now, sitting in his office for the first time since Papa Dee was hospitalized, needing to concentrate on the numbers that Donovan had given him about the expansion into Northern California planned for next year.

"What do you think?" Donovan knocked, asked the question and entered Dexter's office at the same time.

"Looks pretty good so far," Dexter replied, although since he'd been reading the first two sentences for the past ten minutes, he really had no idea.

"What about the idea of opening up a wine-tasting bar in Paradise Valley?"

Dexter nodded slowly. "Sounds like a plan."

"Man, quit with the B.S." He took a seat in one the two leather chairs that faced Dexter's desk. "You probably just started reading the report. And our meeting with Warren and Dad is in an hour."

"Sorry, Don." Dexter tossed the folder on the desk and sat back in his chair. "It's been one of those mornings."

"I know you're worried about Papa Dee, man. We all are. But you were there and heard what the heart specialist said. He assured us that Papa suffered no permanent damage and that there is no inordinate amount of plaque built up in his arteries. So with the medication, change in diet and a little more exercise…he'll be good as new. It's a good thing we had a doctor at the party." Dexter remained silent, staring out the large window that revealed acres and acres of loaded grapevines. "Wait a minute…" Donovan leaned forward, eyeing his brother carefully. "You're not thinking about Papa Dee or his doctors. You're thinking about *her*, that Buckner chick, aren't you?" Donovan chuckled; sat back in his seat. "What's going on, player?"

"Why do you think something is going on?"

"Because it took me a minute to put two plus two together to get four, but now that I have…"

"You're a mathematician? Nothing is going on, bro. Just took her out to dinner, on behalf of the family showing our appreciation and what not."

"Is that so? Our comping her stay one hundred percent wasn't appreciation enough?"

Dexter shrugged. "I wanted to add a personal touch."

"Ha! I'm sure you did."

"Yes, but not in the way you mean. I took her out for a

nice dinner and then delivered her to her door with nothing more than a kiss and a good-night."

"You're joking, right?" Donovan deadpanned. "What, you're not attracted to her?"

"She's not really my type, but it's not that." Dexter's brows creased in thought. "She's different. I know some very intelligent women and—"

"Of course you do," Diamond interrupted, walking in and taking the seat next to Donovan. "You grew up with one."

"He's talking about the doctor," Donovan said.

"At Loma Linda? Which one?"

"No, Dr. Buckner. The woman who helped save Papa Dee."

"Of course! She's female and breathing." Diamond held out the word and winked at Donovan. "Why am I not surprised?"

"Because you know our brother," Donovan said with a sly grin.

Dexter walked over and took a seat at the conference table. "I suggest ya'll get out of my business and into Drake Wines' business. Where's Dad and Warren?"

"Warren is on his way," Diamond replied. "As for Dad, we'll have to go on without him. Looks like Papa Dee might get released a day early. He, Mom and the grands are on their way to the hospital…hopefully to pick him up."

Dexter looked up as Warren Drake entered the room. "Well," he said, giving his cousin a nod as he approached the group. "Let's get started on the discussion about how we're getting ready to take over Napa Valley."

Dexter wasn't the only one buried in work. Faye had vowed not to check her work emails during the week she was at Drake Wines, but a phone call from San Diego

State's School of Nursing had changed all that. After months of correspondence and phone calls, the university had agreed to an educational partnership. A select group of senior students would be able to volunteer at the clinic in exchange for credit toward their degree. With the school year starting shortly, there was no time to waste. Faye accessed her work inbox, found the email and attachments that the school had sent and scanned the histories of the nurses suggested. She also saw emails from the agency through which she'd rented her condominium, saying that it was ready for move-in, and another one from the church that had previously owned the building where the clinic would be housed and had shown charity in selling the place at almost thirty-five percent below market value. So after transferring the information to be printed out in the hotel's business center, she made appointments to visit the condo and the commercial building. Faye smiled, happy to feel back in her element and out of the mood that had enveloped her since last night…and the kiss.

That kiss. That man. Those incredible lips. Faye glanced at the clock and then reached for her phone. As soon as Adeline answered, Faye said, "I'm in trouble."

"Ooh, good! You must have met someone."

"Not just someone, girl," Faye said. Her tone was serious, somber even. "One of the owners of this resort."

Adeline squealed. "Please tell me that your self-imposed celibacy is over."

Sometimes Faye regretted having ever told Adeline about her love life. Or lack thereof. "I can't tell you that because it isn't true. We did go to dinner though."

"Okay, that's a start. What happened afterward?"

"He walked me to my room, gave me a brief kiss and left—just like a gentleman."

"That's it?"

"Don't sound so disappointed."

"Don't mind me, girl. After being married for ten years, I can't imagine going without sex for as long as you. And I can't imagine why you think you're in trouble."

"Because I can't stop thinking about him."

"Ooh, praise the Lord! There's hope for you yet. So tell me about him. Is he handsome? How tall? How old? How'd you meet him? Start at the beginning and don't leave anything out!"

Faye gave her the rundown, from the time she saw him in the lobby until he'd kissed her good-night. "I'd be lying if I said I didn't find him attractive. But we're total opposites. I can't see what we'd have in common."

"He has a penis and you say you're attracted. I can think of at least one thing that you both might like."

"Yeah, right."

"I'm serious! Stop being such a conservative prude and live a little. You're only there for a few more days before moving to San Diego. As you've pointed out, you two are opposites and will probably travel in totally different circles. It is most likely that after you leave the resort, you'll never see him again." That thought didn't sit well with Faye at all. Yes, she was in trouble big-time. "Here, your choices were limited. It made it easy for you to get buried in work. But I worry about you, Faye. You're a pretty girl, an intelligent and skilled doctor. When you finish healing and comforting all of your patients, I want you to have someone in your life who can comfort you."

"It would be nice to have a friend here." Aside from the church group she'd met in Haiti, and the subsequent partnership with the San Diego ministry who'd sold her the building for the clinic, she really knew no one in Southern California.

"Then it's settled. If he asks you out on another date,

you'll go. If he doesn't ask you out, then you ask him. If he agrees, and wants to end the evening in a horizontal position, you'll be open to that. Right?"

"Addie! I just met him. He'll think I'm…easy, promiscuous!"

"This is the twenty-first century and you're not a virgin. He'll think you're a warm-blooded woman with grown-up needs. Promise me if the opportunity arises you'll at least consider what I've said?"

"I promise to *consider* it. But that's all."

Shortly after their conversation, Faye left the resort. She spent a good deal of the day in San Diego: checking out her new condo, seeing the building that would house the clinic and meeting with the pastor of Open Arms Church. Both on the way to and on the way back from San Diego she thought about what her friend Adeline had said.

"That woman is crazy," she finally decided. *Dexter probably has no desire to go out with me again, and I'm definitely not going to ask him out.* "Just focus on the clinic, Faye. That alone will be a full plate."

Just like that, Faye dismissed the notion of again hooking up with Dexter. Soon, she would learn that life was what happened when one was busy making other plans.

Chapter 13

Two days later, the following Monday, Faye had just returned to her room after having lunch in the Grapevine when her hotel phone rang. After two quiet evenings where the landline had remained silent, she'd begun to think that her dinner with Dexter was indeed "one night only" and that if she could simply lie low for the next few days she could leave Drake Wines with fairly good memories—not necessarily those that Adeline suggested, but nice ones nonetheless. Now, she was sure he was calling to try and finish what he'd started. *Probably not every day that he doesn't get the goods.*

"Hello?"

"Dr. Buckner? This is Genevieve Drake."

This was a surprise. I hope Papa Dee is okay. "Yes, Mrs. Drake."

"Please, call me Genevieve. And may I call you Faye?"

"Absolutely."

"I'm sure you have a lot going on, so I'll get right to the point. We brought home Papa Dee today."

"That's good news."

"It is indeed. We thought it would happen a couple days earlier but a low fever kept them cautious. But he's home now and that's why I'm calling. He's asked about you. I thought I'd invite you for tea and then, if you have time, perhaps you could check in on him."

"That's very kind of you, Mrs. Drake—"

"Genevieve."

"Yes, Genevieve. But your family has already done so much. I'll be more than happy to check in on Mr. Drake. It's not necessary to make a fuss by fixing tea."

"It's no fuss—we have tea every day. Besides, my son told me that you've moved here from Haiti to start your own clinic. I think that is a very noble endeavor and would like to hear more about that, and to speak with you about another matter as well. Would three o'clock work for you?"

Faye looked at the desk clock. "That sounds fine."

"Perfect. Our home isn't far from the hotel. I'll meet you in the lobby."

"There are few tea times in Haiti. Is this a formal affair?"

"Oh, heavens no!" Genevieve said, with a chuckle. "Very casual. Wear whatever is comfortable."

It sounded simple enough, but it still took Faye half an hour to decide on a pencil skirt in denim fabric paired with a stark white peasant blouse and leather flats. Her new hairstyle had survived the weekend, but the professional makeup job done in the salon gave way to a hint of blush, lipstick and a spritz of her favorite cologne.

Shortly after Faye arrived there, Genevieve entered the lobby. She was put together from head to toe; shoulder-length black hair held back with a pearl clasp, a light blue

knit shell and navy slacks that complemented her skin tone
and slender frame. They greeted each other and within
minutes were driving in an SUV and passing between two
columns and under a wrought-iron sign that simply read
DRAKE in elegant calligraphy.

"Your property is beautiful," Faye said, looking out on
the picturesque landscaping that appeared to belong on a
movie set.

"Thank you, Faye," Genevieve said. "It's been in the
family for over a hundred years. Donald, my husband,
grew up on this property—and all of our children, of
course. When the boys were young, they'd invite their
friends out and play baseball over there—" she pointed
toward a vast expanse of flat land surrounded by trees
"—or ride horses. Never a dull moment when the kids
were young—or now either for that matter." They came to
a stop in front of a sprawling white house with contrasting
black shutters. "Here we are. Welcome to the Drake estate."

Indeed, Faye thought as she exited the pearl white Es-
calade and looked around her. In addition to what she
assumed was the main house there were three smaller
but similarly designed homes that sat back not far from
a cobblestone connecting road. A fence made of stark
white wood and wrought iron surrounded as much of the
property as she could see, and beyond it were grapevines
and rolling hills, one of which contained the Honeymoon
House, as Faye recalled from the hotel brochure.

They entered the home and, like the outside landscape,
the interior did not disappoint. Light filtered in through
large picture windows, accenting the warm earth tones
mixed with coppers and gold. They bypassed a large room
and continued down the hall to a smaller one, a library as
it turned out. The burgundy, navy and tan color scheme
complemented the cherrywood and included a cozy sit-

ting area with two wingbacks and a love seat. Inside sat another woman who'd thanked her at the hospital.

"You remember my mother-in-law," Genevieve said as they entered.

"Mary Drake," the woman said, her smile warm, her matronly look inviting and familiar.

"Yes, Mrs. Drake."

"Please, baby. Just call me Miss Mary, or Grandma, same as the other kids."

"Thank you, Miss Mary."

A maid entered with an elaborate tea cart. "Faye, how would you like your tea?" Genevieve asked.

"Cream and sugar, please." As Genevieve prepared their tea, Faye continued. "I'm glad to hear about Papa Dee."

"A trooper, that one," Mary said, accepting her teacup and taking a sip.

"The doctors are amazed that his heart is still so strong," Genevieve added, stirring thoughtfully. "But we're worried. That's one of the reasons we wanted to talk to you, Faye. To see if there is any possibility that you could help us where Papa Dee is concerned."

"I'd be happy to help in any way that I can."

"While it looks as though he's on the road to full recovery, we are going to hire a full-time, live-in nurse. We thought that perhaps you could conduct the second interview, ask the types of medical questions necessary to make sure they're a fit."

Faye nodded. "It would be my pleasure. This tea is delicious, by the way."

"It's my favorite. We get it at Sprouts, a local store that carries mostly organic produce. Which is a perfect segue into our second plan of action with Papa. He loves his fried this and smothered that, is a southern boy through and through, but we want to hire a nutritionist who can design a menu befitting his age and health concerns."

"It sounds like you're doing all the right things."

"We're trying," Genevieve said, her rapidly blinking eyes fighting tears. "He means so much to us."

"We understand that you arrived here from Haiti," Mary said. "How did you hear of our resort?"

For the next half hour, Faye gave the short version of her story: the Peace Corps, her time in Africa, how the earthquake brought her back to the western hemisphere and how the kindness and generosity of her mentor had brought her here. "I miss Haiti and the work I did there. But it's good to be back in the States."

The telephone rang. "Excuse me," Genevieve said, reaching for the crystal-beaded cordless. "Hello?" She listened, smiling at Faye as she did so. "Oh, yes. Certainly. We'll come right away. That was the nurse," she said after hanging up. "Papa will be taking his nap soon. She suggested we come now." They both peered at a closed-eyed Mary, looking regal, even in sleep.

"Looks like it's nap time for a few people," Genevieve loudly whispered. They stood to leave. The phone rang again. "Wouldn't you know it? The phone has barely rung all afternoon." She looked at the caller ID. "Ah, this is my cousin from up north. Hello, Benita. I was just heading out. Can I call you back?" Faye noted the beautiful ring Genevieve wore as she waved her right hand. "Oh, okay. I understand. Hold on a moment." She pressed the hold button. "Faye, I need to take this call. Would you mind terribly going to see Papa without me? His is the first house down the lane. There are orange and lemon trees in front, and a swing on the porch. You can't miss it."

"No problem." She held out her hand. "Thanks for the tea."

Faye left the room and, resisting the urge to snoop and check out other parts of the house, was soon outside in the afternoon sun. She enjoyed the short walk to the first of several smaller houses, walked up the curved entrance and used the brass knocker.

The door opened and she looked into the face she least expected to see.

Dexter leaned against the doorjamb. "Well…hello."

Chapter 14

"Hello." He looked better than she remembered. "I understand that Mr. Drake wants to see me?"

"And which Mr. Drake is that?" The smile was hubristic, but it worked.

"Mr. *David* Drake Sr." Faye smiled too. Her flirting skills were rusty, but something about this man made her feel all girlie inside.

Dexter gave her the once-over. "Come on in," he drawled.

He turned and she followed him across a comfortably appointed living room and down a short hall. She checked out his tight butt without shame, drank in his broad shoulders, narrow waist and long legs…and remembered Adeline's nudge to have fun. Once again his firm booty beckoned. *I could have some fun with that.* They reached Papa Dee's bedroom before her mind had a chance to run with just how much fun she could have.

"Someone to see you, Papa," Dexter announced.

Faye walked up to the bed, her smile bright, her countenance genuinely cheerful. "Hello, Mr. Drake," she said, lightly touching his arm. "You look much better than the last time I saw you."

The jovial man whom Faye remembered from the birthday party was not the one she encountered now. He looked at her intensely, his eyes squinting as if he was recalling her presence. His stare was so unflinching and lasted to the point where she became uncomfortable. *Does he not remember me?* she wondered.

Papa Dee slowly raised his hand and placed it on Faye's arm. "There's my curly-haired angel," he said, his voice raspy, his eyes bright. "I thought you'd gone and left me for a younger man."

Faye's smile broadened, and she was surprised to feel tears threatening to fall. "It's so good to see you, Papa," she said, using the name that everyone else did without realizing it. "You look really good."

"I know you're fibbing, sweet pea," he said, his breath slightly labored. "But it sure sounds nice."

"Whatever you say." She placed a thumb on his wrist and checked his pulse with him being none the wiser. She then caressed his cheek, feeling his neck in the process. *No temperature. Good.* "I imagine you're just about ready to get out of that bed."

"About to go stir-crazy."

"I'll check out the doctor's report and talk to the nurse. Let's see if we can get those young bones to moving."

Papa Dee nodded as his eyes fluttered closed. Itching for her stethoscope, Faye instead placed a light hand on his chest, noting that his breathing was full and steady. She looked up and, seeing the concern in his eyes, gave Dexter a reassuring smile. *He's good,* she mouthed. He nodded and motioned for them to leave the bedroom.

They walked into the open-concept living area, where the nurse was typing on her computer. After introducing herself, Faye asked several questions regarding Papa Dee's health, including the medications that had been prescribed and the rehabilitation program that had been established. She found out that the nurse was on loan from the hospital, and would be leaving at week's end. Faye made a mental note to speak with Genevieve tomorrow about a replacement. All of this was handled in the calm, no-nonsense persona she'd adopted while in residency at a hospital in Washington, D.C. and honed in makeshift tents in the bowels of Africa. Dexter looked on with keen interest at a woman obviously in her element and very good at what she did. And was it his imagination, or did she get better looking every time he saw her? He noticed the way her mouth pursed just so when she was thinking and the way her fine hair made wispy curls at her temples, curls he wanted to rub with his finger, in front of ears he wanted to outline with his tongue. Never before had he noticed how there could be such sexiness in simplicity and how not having all of one's assets on full display could awaken his curiosity to the content of her hidden treasures. She was, in a word, different. There was something else. Something he couldn't quite pinpoint, couldn't quite define, drawing him to her despite his inner protestations that she "wasn't his type."

After finishing with the nurse, Faye walked over to where Dexter gazed out the window. "He's recovering nicely," she said, also staring out on the beautiful August afternoon. Palm trees collided with maples in a zany yet effortless landscape, while hummingbirds vied for nectar from the feeders strategically hung from the frame of Papa Dee's front porch. "I think he'll be all right." At this confident statement, Dexter offered Faye an unreadable look. His smoldering eyes sent shivers one place and intense heat another.

To break the spell she felt he was undoubtedly weaving with his sparkling, curly-lash-framed eyes, she looked at her watch and was genuinely surprised at the time. "Oh! I need to run. I signed up for the DD&T that starts at six-thirty."

Dexter's sister, Diamond, had implemented this latest resort offering a year ago. Guests at the hotel were treated to a grand tour of the facilities followed by a discounted dinner at the Grapevine and dancing in the lounge. He'd been totally for it when she presented it to the group, had even participated sometimes by talking to the groups when they came through the cellar or wine shop. But he had no intentions of letting someone else school Faye Buckner on the art of fine wines. No, he planned to do that all by his lonesome.

He grabbed her hand. "Come with me."

The movement was spontaneous and surprising, as evidenced by Faye's gut reaction—to pull away. "What are you doing?"

"You scared of me?"

Wide eyes. Shaky voice. "No."

"Ha! Liar."

Faye's voice hardened. "I've faced down machetes in a war zone. Trust me, you don't scare me."

Dexter nodded, a gleam of appreciation in his eyes. "Then, let's go." Most women fawned over him, considered it a coup just to be in his presence. Few were a challenge, and that hadn't been a problem. Until now. Now he found himself measuring his past conquests against this unexpected love interest. *Wait, did I just think about the L-word? Down, Dexter. Slow your fantasizing roll.*

They walked outside and got into the SUV that Faye had assumed belonged to the nurse. "This your car, too?"

"Yep."

"How many cars do you have?"

"Three."

"How many can you drive at one time?" A look. No answer. "I don't begrudge wealth," Faye continued, almost as if to herself. "I really don't. But living in poverty-stricken nations almost exclusively for the past eight years has changed how I see things. Many people see money in terms of how it can make their own lives better. I see it in terms of how many people I can help."

"*Help* is the operative word. In our way, my family helps people, too. We help them feel better, help them celebrate. We also have several charities that we support. I don't think one type of help is better than another."

"People eating rice for meals may beg to disagree."

"I won't argue that."

"I don't want to argue at all. Sorry, I probably shouldn't have brought it up."

"No worries."

Instead of going to the vineyard, wine store, cellar or any other stops mentioned on the brochure, they drove in front of an office building. "What happens here?" she asked

Dexter smiled. "Magic. Let me get that door for you."

Another gentlemanly act? Faye realized she'd almost forgotten what being with one of them felt like. She exited the car, inhaled Dexter's trademark scent and felt her heart flip-flop in spite of the previous day's resolve, despite her thoughts that he was probably wine country's biggest playboy. While walking with him to the side door he led them to, she tried to remember the last time she felt this way. And realized she was experiencing something that she'd never felt before.

"Welcome to my lab."

He reached for an opened bottle. "This one should be ready to try."

"I probably shouldn't. I'm not much of a drinker, remember? Plus, no offense, but I think wine tastes disgusting."

"Oh, baby!" Dexter placed a hand to his chest. "You wound me! Why don't you tell me how you really feel?" Chuckling at her expression, he continued. "I'm just messing with you. I'm not offended." Her look remained skeptical. "Come on. Just a sip."

"Okay."

He poured a small amount of the deep burgundy liquid into two large wineglasses. "Swirl it, like this," he said, gently moving the liquid around. "Now, take a sniff, like this." He placed the rim of the glass directly under his nose and inhaled deeply. Faye did the same. "What do you smell?"

Faye shrugged. "Wine, I guess."

"No, close your eyes." She did. "Relax, and focus on your olfactory senses."

Faye opened one eye.

"That word means smell," Dexter teased.

Both eyes were now open. "Very cute."

"Yes, you are."

To hide her sudden case of nerves, Faye became very interested in the contents of her glass. She closed her eyes and inhaled deeply. "I think I smell citrus."

"Good. What else?"

"Maybe...spices?"

"Which ones?"

"I don't know."

"Let's taste it." Dexter showed her how to take a sip, let it rest on her palate before swallowing. She mimicked his moves. "Which spice did you taste?"

"I don't know. But I usually don't like wine, and this is good. It's sweet."

"Yes. Just like you."

"Are you always such a flirt?"

"Most times," he admitted, with the crooked, impish smile that she'd come to expect, and quite like. "But I'm always sincere. You seem like a sweet girl. A good girl. Are you?"

"As opposed to a bad girl?" Dexter looked, waited. "I guess so." He continued his intense perusal, his brownish-hazel orbs almost hidden behind long, curly lashes. "Why are you looking at me like that?"

"Because I'm curious about something."

"What?" Faye asked, totally aware that she was entering uncharted territory at her own risk.

"I wonder if the wine tastes the same on your lips as it does on mine."

He leaned forward. She leaned back. "How do you mix the, uh, spices and citrus?" she asked, flustered and fluttering at the same time.

He pulled back, noting her skittishness and the wild way her pulse was beating in her neck. "There are no additives, sweetheart. It's all in what type of grape is used, and the fermenting process."

"Oh."

"Any more questions before I kiss you? I can kiss you, can't I?"

Dexter took her silence as consent. When his lips touched hers, Faye would later swear that the earth shook ever so slightly. Or was it her body? Of its own volition, her body leaned forward for more of this bliss. He obliged, pressing more firmly this time, placing a possessive hand at the small of her back, bringing her closer. The groan that erupted from her throat was foreign to her ears, as was this almost feral need to touch this man. She opened her mouth, welcoming his deepening of the kiss even as she wrapped her arms around the shoulders she'd earlier admired. Tongues swirled, hardened nipples pressed against a strong chest, hands explored. Dexter lightened his touch, rained kisses on her neck, cheek and forehead, and, for a delicious mind-boggling second, nibbled on her ear. He pulled away to find Faye more unreserved than he'd ever seen her—eyes closed, mouth slack—and decided that he quite liked her in this uninhibited state.

"Interesting."

Faye's eyes fluttered open. "What?"

"The taste. I think it's even better on your lips."

"Oh, right. The wine."

Dexter's chuckle was deep and knowing. "This is a portion of the Drake Wines operation that is not a part of the public tour. So know that you're special."

"I am?" Faye was genuinely surprised.

"You don't know?"

The tour continued then, not only with the spots that Faye expected—the wine store, cellar, vineyard and such—but also with the Honeymoon House, shown with a delightful narrative from Dexter about Papa Dee's colorful upbringing and the stables that housed the most beautiful horses that Faye had ever seen. An hour after they'd left Papa Dee's, he again dropped her off at her room's door.

"Thanks for the tour," she said, looking at those delectable lips and sounding more breathy than she'd intended.

"Thanks for the kiss."

Faye missed him even before he was gone. The way he'd kissed her had been magical. "Probably lots of practice," she mumbled as she closed the door and plopped down on the sofa. "Why are you doing this?" she asked the empty room. "He's just a heartbreak waiting to happen."

Even as she told herself this, Adeline's words wafted into her mind. *Stop being such a conservative prude and live a little.* With her lips still tingling from his touch, this sounded like a great idea.

Chapter 15

The following day Dexter was working in his lab, deep into perfecting a merlot/cabernet/pinot blend. So much so that he didn't hear the door to the lab open.

"Looks like Papa Dee has a new girlfriend," Donovan said as he entered.

"Who, the nurse?"

"No, the doctor." This got Dexter's attention. "I just passed by his house and saw her and Papa Dee swinging on his porch like old pals."

Dexter smiled, pleased to know that Faye was spending time with his favorite person on earth. "Papa likes 'em young."

"And pretty," Donovan added.

"A married man such as yourself shouldn't be knowing too much about what the good doctor looks like." Dexter's casual air belied the thoughts whirling in his mind.

"Nothing wrong with looking, brother. Your eyes don't stop working because you get married. You'll see."

"No I won't. Diamond is getting ready to give Mama her first grandchild, and I'm sure you and Marissa are working on the second. I think being the favorite uncle and perpetual bachelor suits me just fine."

"You say that now. I did, too. But when you meet the right woman, everything changes."

"I can't see myself with just one woman, man."

Donovan leaned against the counter, watching his brother in his element, doing what he loved. "So you're going to be one of those pitiful-looking brothers sporting gray whiskers and still chasing skirts?" He continued, laughing as he imagined the words he said. "A beer gut over your belt, high-water pants and a baseball cap on backward trying to recapture your youth?"

"You know I'm not going out like that. I never wore my hat backward when that was in vogue. As for flab and rolls and ill-fitting clothes, that won't happen in this lifetime. I'm going to be like Pops…with lady friends till the end."

They were silent a moment, both thinking about the party and the little tiff that happened when Birdie wanted to dance with Papa Dee but he chose to dance with Charlotte. "I have to give it to him," Donovan said. "That man is something."

"Yes, he is."

"I know he's lived longer than most, but I'm not ready to lose him."

"The world won't be the same without him in it, that's for sure." After corking the blend he'd been working on, Dexter walked over to a large refrigerator and took out a sparkling wine taster pack: four different bottles of wine packaged in a carton.

"Hot date tonight?" Donovan asked.

"You might say that."

"Do I know her?"

"A little, but you definitely know him. I'm going to cook dinner for Pops," Dexter continued, in answer to Donovan's quizzical look. "And invite Faye to join us."

"I don't know, man. You're pretty popular with the ladies, but she doesn't seem the type to want to play that game."

"Oh, she definitely wants to play. She just might not know yet just how much."

As soon as his brother left, Dexter closed up shop to get the plan he'd formulated under way, the one hatched somewhere between talk of Papa, parties and pretty women swinging with his great-grandpa. It was true. Dexter didn't see himself with just one woman. But tonight he did envision himself with one woman in particular. He hoped she was at the hotel, and that she was hungry.

Ten minutes after he'd arrived at Papa Dee's and given the nurse a couple of hours off, he called Faye.

"Hello?"

"Can you cook?"

"Dexter?"

"No, Bobby Flay." Faye laughed. "Yes it's me, woman. Now answer the question."

A slight hesitation and then, "I can cook a little bit."

"Good. Have you eaten?"

"No, not yet."

"Then the pleasure of your company is being requested at Papa Dee's. Should I get someone to bring you over?"

"I don't recall accepting your invitation yet."

"This one is in the bag, baby. You might turn me down but there is no way you'll say no to a one-hundred-year-old man whose tomorrow is not promised."

"That's low, Dex."

He heard the smile in her voice and knew the evening

was unfolding just the way he'd imagined. "Don't hate the player, baby. Hate the game."

Before long, Faye was knocking on Papa Dee's screen door. "Hello!"

"It's open!" Dexter replied from the kitchen. "Come on in." He heard the door open and close. "I'm in the kitchen."

Faye followed the sounds of pots and utensils rattling and was soon in Papa Dee's small yet functional kitchen.

"Wow." Once again a word meant to be spoken silently was uttered out loud. What about this man kept giving her leave of her senses? She tried to divert her eyes, make it look as though she were referencing the decor, but Dexter's face told her that he'd already seen her stare. She couldn't help it. There was absolutely no way a man (or any human for that matter) should look so good in jeans and an apron. Sexy didn't begin to describe how the jeans cupped his butt and how the apron ties drew one's attention to his narrow waist and broad back. His turning around did her no favors. His stark white shirt was unbuttoned to reveal a solid, bare chest; the sleeves rolled up to show arms Faye knew would feel just right around her shoulders. "What I meant to say was," she began in an attempt at face saving, "is that something smells good in here."

Dexter leaned against the fridge. "Haven't started cooking yet, so it must be me."

Faye glanced over at the stove. Indeed, the skillet on one of the burners was empty and the pot on one of the back burners contained only water. "Maybe it's the vegetables," she continued with a nod to the onions, carrots, garlic, celery and other items on the cutting board. "I find their raw state intoxicating." To further prove her point, she walked over, picked up an onion and inhaled deeply. "Yes, this is what I smelled. Yum."

Her look challenged him to not believe her. His look

said she was full of bull. The sexual tension that erupted every time they saw each other dissipated. They burst out laughing.

"Salad or sauce?" Dexter walked over to the counter and took the onion out of Faye's hand.

"What?"

"Would you like to make the salad, or the sauce?"

Since the only pasta sauce Faye had ever made simply involved opening a jar and heating the contents in a saucepan, her choice was easy. "Salad."

"Knives are in that drawer," Dexter said, reaching to pull another cutting board from the cupboard. "Salad fixings are in the fridge, lower shelf."

She retrieved lettuce, red cabbage, grape tomatoes and peppers, placing them on the cutting board opposite Dexter. As she reached for her knife, she heard the rat-ta-tat-tat sound of knife meeting cutting board with skilled precision. She turned and found Dexter dicing onions, fast and furious, with the skill of a host on a cooking channel.

Is there nothing that this guy can't do well? Faye had never spent much time in the kitchen, had never given cooking much thought at all. Hers was a simple palate, often assuaged by whatever food was being prepared en masse. "How do you do that?"

Dexter looked over his shoulder and saw Faye's eyes on the knife. "What…this?" After making horizontal and vertical slits with the knife, he created perfectly proportioned diced pieces of onions in a matter of seconds.

"Did you take cooking lessons?" Faye was genuinely amazed.

"At the elbow of my mother, grandmother and Papa Dee. It's not as hard as it looks. Here, let me show you."

"No, that's okay."

"Come on, Doctor. I'd think you'd be very skilled with

a knife." He walked over to her board. "Turn around." She did, and he stood behind her. Close. Way too close. Wrapping his arms around her, he picked up the knife and placed it in her hands.

And I'm supposed to think with your arms wrapped around me? And your hard chest pressing against my back? Seriously, Dexter? Seriously?

"Okay," he said, his breath precariously close to her temple. "Slice the peppers like this." With her small hand enveloped by his much larger one, they made the cuts. "Now, place the tip of the knife on the cutting board and move the knife up and down as you push the vegetable forward...like this."

"You're a good teacher," Faye murmured, almost giddy from the smell of his cologne and the feel of her body wedged between his body and the counter.

"Uh-huh." He pressed his body up against hers, so that there was no mistaking the slow, deliberate grinding motion against her buttocks. "Later on, I have another lesson I'd like you to learn."

Faye gripped the knife. Her breathing lightened and her kitty meowed. If she didn't do something fast, she'd throw caution, common sense and decorum to the wind and take this hunk of goodness right here on his great-grandfather's kitchen floor. She managed to turn around within the tight confines of his chest and the counter. Her intent was to push him away. Her arms had other plans. They reached up, totally in defiance of her original intention, and wrapped themselves around Dexter's neck, even as she lifted her head and he lowered his and their mouths met in a blissful reunion that had been a little more than twenty-four hours in the making. Way too long. Their tongues touched and twirled, sensations exploding inside her mouth. Faye followed Dexter's lead as he teased the tip of her tongue with the tip of his. His stiff tongue plunged back inside her warm, hot mouth, even as a hand slid up to tease the already hardened nipple pressing against her simple tank top. He slid his hand down her back. She shivered, even as a volcano of passion erupted inside her. Who knew it even existed? Where was the calm, conservative doctor, Faye wondered, and who was this tigress ready to relieve this man she kissed of his clothes?

"Mmm." She moaned her agreement in his deepening the kiss. He slid quick pecks along her jaw and neck before coming back to reclaim her mouth again. For both of them, all senses save those of touch and feel were blocked out, so caught up were they in this moment of unbridled ardor.

He slid his hand between them, inside the lacy bra covering her chocolate treasures. He tweaked her nipple. And then...and then...

Papa Dee, who'd been watching for a second or two, spoke. "Go on, son. Show that gal what you're working with!"

Chapter 16

"Pops!" Dexter turned his head, but didn't immediately separate from the object of his affection.

"Mr. Drake!" Faye did what she'd initially planned when turning around in the first place. She pushed Dexter away and straightened her clothes. "I, uh, came to check on you!"

"Checking on the wrong mister, looks like." The twinkle in his eye could have rivaled the planet Venus.

"Get on in here, Pops, and stop embarrassing the lady. You were supposed to be napping until dinner was done."

"Wasn't no sharing what y'all were cooking up. Hehehe." He walked over to the cupboard, retrieved olive oil and poured some into the skillet. "Throw those onions in here and get to working on the rest of those vegetables. I'm hungry!"

Under Papa Dee's watchful eye and instruction, a mouth-watering meal of pasta and meatballs soon graced the table, along with Faye's salad—topped with fresh mozzarella and Papa Dee's special apple cider vinaigrette. They ate, laughed, listened to tales of Papa Dee's youth and the women who loved him...and sampled sparkling wine.

"This is wine?" Faye had asked, after sampling the fruity rosé Dexter placed before her to accompany the salad. "It's delicious!"

"Careful, baby girl. It tastes good but make no mistake—those grapes are well fermented."

"Meaning?"

Dexter looked at Papa Dee, who smiled. "Never mind," he said, pouring more bubbly into her glass.

The sampling continued with a rare sparkling red served during the entrée and the dessert wine that Faye had previously enjoyed paired with Grandma Mary's pound cake. During this time the nurse returned, and Papa Dee retired for the evening.

"I love Papa Dee," Faye exclaimed when Dexter had returned from saying good-night. Her eyes were bright and her tone was animated. "Makes me miss my grandpa. Didn't see much of him and Grandma after my mom remarried and we moved to Saint Louis." She turned to Dexter. "Have you ever seen a cow up close?" Her hand bumped his arm. "Oh, my. Your arms are big!" Her volume increased with each sentence, and she started to giggle.

"Okay, Doctor. I think it's time to get you back to your room." He stood and moved to help her up.

"Please, Dexter, I'm not an invalid," she said, swatting away his hand and trying to rise. Unfortunately, her motor skills were lubricated. "Ooh." Another giggle. "Oh, my goodness," she drawled, now leaning against Dexter and looking up dreamily into his eyes. "I think I'm a bit tipsy."

"I think you're right."

He sat—translated, *poured*—her into the passenger seat, and five minutes later had her snuggled against his side as they walked through the lobby to the elevator. Using a special key, Dexter summoned a car in an instant, and as soon as it arrived they were whisked directly to Faye's floor.

"Really, I'm okay. I can walk. My head was just woozy for a minute."

"I know you're stone-cold sober. I just like how you feel in my arms."

"I like how you feel, too. How you look, how you—" she took a deep whiff of his shirt "—smell."

Dexter gave Faye a look out of the side of his eye. *Ms. Conservative. You are going to be some kind of embarrassed tomorrow. But I'm liking what I'm seeing tonight.* They reached the door. "Where is your card?"

Faye retrieved it from her purse and, since he'd requested it the first two times, gave Dexter the card to open the door. He did, and she promptly put her hand on his arm. "I want you to come inside."

This was a switch. The other two times she'd barely left enough space for her to squiggle through the opening before closing the door. He followed her inside.

"I need to lie down for just one minute. Come join me."

"You're a lightweight. I should have listened." Dexter felt bad for giving her wine that she drank like soda. "I'll order up some coffee for you. And water. You're probably dehydrated."

"I am not dehydrated. I am in full control of my facilities and have made a decision." Dexter thought, *faculties,* but, okay. She walked over to the bed and plopped on it. "Come. Sit." He did. She turned to face him. "My friend Addie says that I've been working way too hard. She's right. I need to have some fun. I'd like to have some with you."

"We had fun this evening, Doctor. Dinner was nice.

We laughed and talked. Now it's time for you to get some sleep." Even as he said this, Dexter was more than a little aware of how Faye's hand was sliding up and down his leg, sending a burning sensation through his thick denim jeans. Not being made of stone, he decided it was about time to get moving.

"No!" She grabbed his hand. "Sit." He did. Again. "I know you think it's the wine, but it's not. Okay, maybe it's made me a little more forward."

You think?

"But maybe that's best. Because it allows me to say what I've been thinking since I met you. I'd like for us to have sexual intercourse."

"Sexual intercourse?!"

"Yes, Dexter. That is when a penile erection is placed into the—"

"I know what it is, Faye." He stood and pulled back the covers. "Come on," he said, reaching for her foot and taking off her sandal. He always was a sucker for nice feet and toes, and hers were silky, the fresh French pedicure making his mouth water. He made quick work of pulling off her other sandal and fluffing the pillows. "Get under the covers."

"Only if you get under them with me."

"The sooner you get to sleep," he said, continuing to ignore her, "the sooner you'll wake up and realize that you've let the cat out of the proverbial bag."

"Speaking of cats," she said, reaching for her zipper.

"No, you don't." He stayed her hand. "Wait until I leave."

"I don't want you to leave." Her pout was just too perfect for him to ignore. "I want you to stay. Please?"

"Okay, I'll stay. But only if you go to sleep."

"Yes, let's sleep together." She scooted over to make

room for him. Against his better judgment, he lay down. She rolled over and was on him before he could put up a defense."

"I'm so horny. Let's have sex."

"You're drunk. Let's sleep."

And that's what they did.

Chapter 17

Morning came, announced by bright shards of sunlight streaming through the open blinds.

"Argh!" Faye hurried to turn away from the intruding glare. And bumped up against…*a body? Wait, where am I?* She opened her eyes. *Uh-oh.*

Two smiling eyes were staring back at her. "Good morning."

"What are you doing in my room?"

"You insisted that we sleep together. I obliged you."

Her eyes widened. "Did we…" She yanked back the sheet that covered her. Tank top and pants were still on. *Good. I think.*

"No, Doctor. We didn't have the sexual intercourse that you demanded." His broad smile indicated what fun he was having.

"I know that I drank a lot. But you're pulling my leg. There is no way I would ask for, let alone demand, such a thing."

"You could and you did. Your exact words had to do with...how did you say it? Penile erection."

"No!" She pulled the sheet over her head.

It wasn't enough to drown out Dexter's laughter. "I think I got a chance to see the real Faye Buckner last night." She groaned. "Oh, no. Please don't be embarrassed. I really like her."

She closed her eyes. Memories came rushing back. Pasta and wine at Papa Dee's. Sparkling wine. Delicious wine. Too much wine. "Oh, no." She unburied her head and glared at him, too stunned to be embarrassed. "You knew what you were doing. That wine was delicious. You planned for me to drink too much!"

"Baby, if I'd planned to spend the night in your bed, we would be naked right now."

"I can't believe this," she whispered to herself, massaging her forehead as she did so.

Dexter reached out and ran a light hand down her arm. "You don't have a headache, do you?"

"Surprisingly, no."

"Not surprisingly. You were drinking the good stuff." A pause and then, "I'm aching though."

She turned to face him, feeling awkward and strangely comfortable at the same time. Other women might prefer flowery prose and false promises. This straightforward approach allowed her to think with her head, not her heart. For a practical person, it felt better and made sense. "Do I dare ask why?"

"Because I've been lying next to you all night...feeling your leg thrown over my thigh, smelling your scent." Faye swallowed. "Remembering what you said you wanted me to do to you. Do you remember?"

Faye shook her head. "Not really."

"Papa Dee says that a drunk mouth speaks a sober mind." Silence. "Given the sobriety of this new day, would you still like to have sexual intercourse? Or, as I'd prefer to describe it, would you like to make love? For the record, I'd very much like to do so."

Faye sat up against the headboard. "I'd imagine you like to do so quite often."

"I'm a strong, viral, healthy male. Make no mistake about that. But I am also discriminating. I wouldn't make love to just anyone."

"As much as I prefer this to lies and nonsense, it's interesting that we're sitting here discussing sex like I would a medical procedure. It's crazy, actually!"

"I'm sure Addie would agree." Faye almost gave herself whiplash with the quickness of her movement. "Your best friend? You mentioned her last night."

"That's it." Faye threw back the covers and jumped out of bed. "I'm going to take a shower. I need to clear my head."

"Want me to join you?" No answer. Dexter chuckled.

Until a second later when she said softly, "Yes."

"You sure?" he asked, his voice low and soft when he'd entered the bathroom.

"Not really…but I'm not sure I'll ever be this vulnerable, or this bold, again."

"I only want to do this if you want it."

"It's been awhile," she said with a sigh.

"How long?" The head shake was barely noticeable. "On second thought, maybe this isn't such a good idea. I don't want to hurt you."

"Actually, that's probably why you're the right choice. One, I really don't know you, and what I do know of you implies that you are a ladies' man. I know not to take this seriously—that this is physical, nothing more. Two, in a few days I'll leave the resort. I probably won't see you again. And three, you look like someone who practices often and—" she turned away, pulling her tank top over her head "—are probably very good at what you do." Perhaps it was her medical background and intense study of the human body, but as sexually conservative as she was, Faye had never been particularly modest. So with that said, she pulled down her jeans, turned on the showerhead and stepped inside. "Wait," she said, when Dexter began to undress. "Do you have a condom?"

"Yes."

"Good. Come on in."

Dexter frowned. He enjoyed straightforwardness as much as the next person, but Faye's approach was too clinical, too detached. *She wants to dictate what happens here.* As he removed his jeans and boxers, he knew that *that* wasn't going to happen.

Faye knew the moment Dexter stepped into the stall. Goosebumps broke out all over her body though she hadn't been touched. *Best to stay focused and in control.* "Dexter, can you grab the soa—"

Kisses on her buttocks were not at all what she'd expected.

She froze.

He chuckled.

"Just relax," he murmured. "And enjoy."

The dream! Her shivering began in earnest now; her mind scrambled amid the strange sensations and surprises. "Wait…"

"Shh…don't talk. Feel." Sometime in the past few seconds, he'd managed to grab the sponge. Her logical mind wondered how he could have done that when his tongue had been…*oh, well.* Never mind thinking. Just managing to stay upright on legs resembling noodles was a tall order.

Turns out she didn't have to. As water chased the suds away, Dexter placed his hands around her waist, lifting her off the ground. Her legs automatically wrapped around his hips, leaving her open and exposed. *Wanton. Wicked.* Securing her against the shower wall, he began an oral assault—kissing her shoulder, neck, nibbling her earlobe, before slanting his mouth over hers and initiating a bruising kiss. Her back felt the cool of the marble, the heat of the water and Dexter's tongue searching, swirling as his hips mimicked its movement. Her nipples pebbled into hardened buds as he slid a hand along her side, briefly caressing her hip before sliding his hand between them, teasing her lower set of lips the way his mouth did her upper ones. Soon another nub was hardened, the slick wetness between her legs having nothing to do with the fact that they were in the shower. Over and again he slid a strong middle finger between her folds, setting up a rhythm that Faye's hips immediately began to pattern. Encased in a fog of passion, she became aware of a strange mewling sound. It took several seconds to realize that she was the source. When the finger that had stroked her into madness delved inside her, she came undone, enjoying a release unlike she'd ever experienced, her fingernails sinking into Dexter's shoulders as she tried to hold onto sanity.

Slowly easing her down from the wall, Dexter led Faye from the shower and patted her dry. He'd been surprised at the tightness he encountered, believing that she wasn't a virgin only because she'd earlier told him so. But he was determined to rock her world in a way that she would never forget, and in doing so, he knew he'd have to be a patient man. Fortunately for both of them, time was on their side. Dexter hadn't finished what he'd come to her room to do. He was just getting started.

Chapter 18

"How are you feeling?" he whispered, patting the last vestiges of water off Faye's skin and enveloping her in a smoldering hug.

"That was pretty amazing," she admitted. "But I'm sure you get told that often."

"Right now isn't about what others tell me. Right now is all about you." With that, he reached for a bottle of lemon-scented oil, lifted her off the ground and walked purposefully toward the bed. Faye's eyes never left his as he gingerly placed her on the king-size masterpiece, unscrewed the cap on the bottle and poured a generous amount into his hand. "When is the last time you had a massage?"

"The day of Papa Dee's party. I chose the shiatsu massage offered at the salon."

"Good choice," he said, briskly rubbing his hands together to heat his palms and the oil. "I think you'll like this one much better." After smoothing the oil down the length of her legs, he reached for the foot he'd earlier admired and began a slow, rhythmic kneading. Using his basic knowledge of reflexology, he placed his fingers on certain points of her feet, massaging lightly in some places, harder in others, and giving each toe its own special attention. Faye's eyes fluttered closed. Which is why she was totally unprepared for what she felt next—Dexter's skilled tongue circling her toes before sucking the big one into his mouth. She hissed and grabbed fistfuls of sheet, even as her love button quivered with desire.

The massage continued, slow and specific, as his hands performed magic from her ankles to her thighs. He bypassed her pulsating paradise, retrieved more oil, and continued rubbing away kinks and tension, although given the enormity of her orgasm, Faye was certain there was little stress left!

"Turn over."

She complied, and soon her back was receiving the same attention her legs, arms and chest had received. When he began to knead her booty, she thought she'd go wild, and when his tongue replaced the fingers touching seemingly forbidden places, she gave up all pretense of rationality. When he coaxed her to her knees and then slid his face beneath her, lapping her feminine nectar with his tongue, holding her hips firmly in place and maintaining the pressure when she tried to escape his tantalizing torture, tears of ecstasy cascaded down her face and she was not ashamed. He licked her leisurely, purposely, unrelentingly. Even as he did so he slid a finger along her backside, until she felt she'd faint from the pleasure. And when once again the joy of her climax bubbled over into an explosion of sensations, Dexter quickly and expertly sheathed himself and took a slow, steady plunge into her wetness—before she could think and be aware, while she was relaxed and still floating on an orgasmic cloud.

Once they were joined in the most intimate of ways, where not even air could come between them, he stopped. Waited. Allowed her muscles to relax until he was fully accommodated. Until he felt Faye's hips began a timeless dance. Only then did he join her, matching her rhythm, pushing himself deeper, pulling out to the tip, and then plunging back in once, twice, a million times. Faye wasn't sure. All she knew was that what she felt was new and magical and something she wanted to last forever. The rhythm was unpredictable—at times slow and methodical, and then, without warning, a pumping frenzy. Faye simply hung on for the ride, matching stroke for stroke, riled to a point past thinking or caring. Searching for yet another explosion into orbit and when again it finally arrived, they took it together. Dexter moaned deeply, clutching Faye against his heart. Faye screamed, a sound new and foreign to her ears, and collapsed against him.

"How was that for sexual intercourse?" he mumbled, turning them on their sides and spooning her close.

"Just what the doctor ordered," she drawled amid a yawn. And then she fell into one of the deepest sleeps she'd ever known, plagued only by the dream that lay beside her.

Chapter 19

When Faye awoke, Dexter was gone. She rolled over and found a note on his now-cold pillow, written on the elegant stationery the hotel provided:

Hey, Pretty Lady:

I hope you don't have plans for the evening. I'll be by to pick you up at six. Wear those raggedy jeans and T-shirt you had on when arriving at our luxury hotel. J

Dex

Faye couldn't help but smile. She had arrived looking pretty tacky. That day she hadn't given much consideration to where she was going and was more dressed in the mode of where she had been. In the tent cities and countryside of Haiti, clothes were given very little consideration. People were way more concerned about water and food.

Speaking of food, Faye found herself ravenous. The activities of the morning had worked up quite an appetite. She rolled out of bed and was immediately assaulted with the soreness that had resulted from the couple's strenuous acts. "Well, Addie. The cootchie cobwebs are certainly gone." Thinking of her best friend made Faye smile. *The things I've done, she will not believe!*

After ordering room service and then spending an afternoon on the computer, making appointments for the following week and final plans for the benefit fundraiser, Faye went downstairs to meet Dexter. Given what she was wearing, she had not a clue what surprises the evening held. He was in the lobby, talking on one phone and texting on another, looking absolutely dashing in a plain shirt and faded jeans. Faye could do nothing but shake her head. Three cars? Two phones? Movie-star looks. Their worlds were so different. Still, one thing they had in common could not be denied: passion. Pure and simple. The conservative Dr. Buckner possessed an inner freak. No one was more surprised than Faye, nor one more pleased.

"Where are we going?" she asked, after Dexter had surprised her once again by bypassing all of the vehicles in the parking lot and stopping at a golf cart.

"Fishing."

Faye's look could have gone next to the word *incredulous* in the dictionary. "You're kidding, right?" He nodded toward the backseat, where she saw two portable fishing rods, a tackle box, duffle bag and a cooler. "*You*...are going to catch a fish."

"One of us better, or tonight we'll starve." She continued to look at him as one would an alien from Mars. "We're catching our dinner."

Faye was stunned into silence. This man was simply complex, and she was forgetting all about her vow to keep this a totally physical interaction. "You're not what I imagined," she said, at last.

"What? Didn't think a brother like me could get his hands dirty?"

"Not at all. The man I saw when I arrived at the hotel lobby was one who'd balk at crud found beneath his fingernails, as one who gets as many beauty treatments as any female—manicures, pedicures, facials, the works."

"What's wrong with that?" Dexter asked, purposely looking at his perfectly buffed nails.

Belatedly, Faye realized her error. "I didn't mean that as an insult. It's just that your many sides intrigue me."

"As a boy, I was Papa Dee's shadow. He's the one responsible for my country side. We'd hunt and fish and go horseback riding. He loves everything about this land, and passed that down to me. I practically lived in flannels and dungarees until I was ten."

"Dungarees? Ha!"

"That's what an inordinate amount of time spent in the presence of an old man will do," Dexter said with a smile. "Also, don't be surprised if I'm fixing to fetch something, or if you become a gal instead of a woman, or if I ask ever so politely for a bit more of that poontang."

Faye's laughter rang across the mountains, complemented by Dexter's deep chuckle and the sound of the wind.

They reached a nice-size pond about a mile from the commercial property. In the distance beyond, Faye saw the horses, stables and a large red barn they'd passed on her earlier tour. It was a picture right out of a book or magazine: deep, thick grass; endless blue skies; large, fluffy cumulous clouds; and mountains that kissed the heavens. "All of this belongs to you?" she asked, as the golf cart came to a stop.

"All of this belongs to the family," he corrected. "It can be parceled for various buildings, such as what happened when my sister got married and they built their home. But it can never be legally divided or sold outside the family. This will always be Drake territory."

He continued the history lesson on the land and the family that owned it as he unloaded the cart and set them up on a small deck that extended about five feet into the pond. "You ever fish before?"

"Once or twice," Faye responded.

"Lures or live bait?"

"Mostly live," she said, with a cocky smile.

"Nice. I don't have to worry about you going all girlie on me when I pull out the worms." Dexter reached for the tackle box, happy for seemingly no reason. And then it hit him. This was the first time he'd shared his love of nature, specifically fishing, with a woman. None of the women he'd dated, and there had been scores, had ever had the slightest interest regarding the land—except trying to set up residence there. His ex-girlfriend Maria was the only one who'd ridden a horse, and she loved it. But even she scoffed at anything that would ruin her designer jeans. Now here he'd met a woman who could match him stroke for stroke in bed *and* bait a hook? Donovan's words rushed to the forefront of his mind. *When you meet the right woman, everything changes.* Dexter immediately shook off the thought. He wasn't the type who would ever get married. But if he did, he decided, it would probably be to someone like Faye.

Faye leaned against the deck railing and looked out over the sparkling water. "What kinds of fish are stocked in your pond?"

"Perch, bluegill, a few largemouth bass."

"No catfish?"

"You eat those scavengers?"

"Heck, yes! Give me some fried catfish fillets, coleslaw and French fries, and I'm good to go."

"And here I was beginning to think you were a true country girl."

"What's more country than catfish?"

He handed her a baited rod, and with a quick kiss to the lips now pursed in concentration said, "You'll see."

They fished and talked, and Faye found it fascinating that the same man who'd regaled her with talk of college exploits and career achievements in a swanky, upscale restaurant was now equally as comfortable talking about loading a twelve-gauge shotgun, or using horse dung in the making of composted fertilizer for the family garden. She squealed when she reeled in the first catch: a yellowy perch, weighing about two pounds. About ten minutes later, Dexter snagged a four-pound bass. His eyes danced, and she imagined the little boy he'd spoken of, who bragged about his first ten-pound catch for over a week.

After reeling in another nice-sized catch, Dexter walked over to the duffle bag. "You ever clean a fish?" he asked, over his shoulder.

"Sure have," Faye was proud to reply. "Only once though, and actually my grandfather cleaned it. I mostly watched." She watched in silent wonder as Dexter pulled contents from the bag: a skillet, fish grill, plastic plates and various utensils, including a large knife. From a smaller bag inside the larger one came a woven blanket, paper towels and sanitizer. "Are we going to cook out here?"

"Unless you want sushi." He walked to the cart and retrieved the cooler. Placing it on the ground, he pulled out a jug of water and a bottle of sparkling wine, before standing to give Faye her cooking instructions. "Start the side dishes while I handle the fish. Cut the potatoes as thinly as possible, and don't skimp on the olive oil, else we'll be here all night." When she continued to stand there dumbfounded, he added, "There's corn in there, too. Grab those ears and get to shuckin', gal. The sun will be down soon!"

"Normally the doctor gives the orders," she said in response to his demand.

"Not on this land, baby girl," he replied matter-of-factly. "Here, I run things."

It was the best meal she'd ever eaten, especially the simply grilled, lightly seasoned fish, which quickly replaced cornmeal-battered catfish as her new favorite. *Especially when gut, cut and cooked by a fine, shirtless brother.* He'd taken his shirt off while cleaning the fish and so far hadn't bothered to put it back on. The view was fine with Faye, and so was the ambiance. Dexter had remembered everything, even the iPhone that now played smooth music through portable speakers. It was almost as though she were back in Africa with the Peace Corps or her medical team, who on more than one occasion had sat around a campfire on which food had been prepared, listening to the sounds of nature and enjoying the simple life.

They enjoyed a quiet, companionable moment, both lost in their thoughts. Finally, Dexter got up and retrieved the wine. "Now time for dessert," he said, deftly popping the cork, holding himself up with his elbow as he lay back.

"Where are the glasses?" Faye asked, the sudden desire in his eyes sending a squiggle of fire that began in her belly before traveling south.

"Don't worry." Dexter reached for her arm, motioning for her to lie down beside him. "We won't be needing those."

Chapter 20

"Take off your clothes," Dexter demanded, following a leisurely kiss.

"Here? Now?" Even as she asked the question, Faye reached for the zipper on her jeans. "What if someone sees us?"

"No one comes on this part of the property. It's just the two of us."

He quickly stripped out of his clothes, then helped her remove her jeans. A black lacy bra and matching thong quickly followed. "Um, just lay back. Let me look at you. I like your body, baby." He plucked a piece of grass and began to lightly run it over her skin. She shivered. He smiled. "This morning, I had to rush things a bit. Tonight, I plan to take my time."

"I didn't…feel you were…rushing," Faye managed to eke out, as he gently pushed her legs apart and continued his assault. He stroked her nub with the blade, all the while running his fingers up and down her legs, across her stomach, up to her already taut nipples. No matter what happened later, Faye knew that she would never look at grass the same ever again! Dexter picked up the bottle of sparkling wine. "Here, take a sip." His voice was low, deep, commanding; his massive dick bobbed and weaved with a life of its own. She rose up and drank from the bottle, not breaking eye contact with Dexter as he gently poured the ambrosia into her mouth. He moved his hand, and the liquid spilled across Faye's body.

"Aw!"

"Ooh, sorry," he murmured, bowing his head. "Let me get that." He began a journey with his tongue, following the trickle of wine running down her skin. He feasted on her nipples—licking, tugging, biting—until they were hardened peaks. More wine flowed and he stroked her stomach, his tongue stiff in some moments, soft in others; he seemed to know exactly how to ebb and flow. He poured wine near her navel. It tickled. She laughed. When he spread her legs and again reached for the bottle, she grabbed his hand. "No, you can't go there."

His eyes darkened even further. "I can. And I will." He parted her folds with his fingers and teased her pearl. "Unless you don't want it." He stopped. She squirmed. "Do you?"

She nodded, slowly at first and then more feverishly.

"Then tell me. I want to hear you tell me what you want."

"Please..." She reached for his hand, trying to force him to continue.

"No, Doctor. You've expert knowledge of the body. Tell me exactly what you'd like me to do to you."

"I want you to lick my clitoris," Faye panted. "Now!"

Dexter chuckled. Cool wine gave temporary relief to

her raging heat, but not for long. Soon, he had his tongue all over her, adding a C, D, E and F to what was more commonly known as the G-spot. Fingers played a melody within her, drowning out the song's lyrics of loving and wanting and holding on. Instinctively, her hips began to grind in a circular motion, her head swung from side to side and her hands moved back and forth against his hair.

"That's right, baby. Let go. Give this to me." He blew on her wetness and this surprising act, combined with the wind swirling around her naked body, gifting her with nature's embrace, was almost her undoing. She cried out, her hips lifted off the ground, and the stars she saw had nothing to do with the ones overhead.

Rubbing his body against her, he caught her mouth in a searing kiss. The essence of her sweetness mixed with the fruitiness of the wine was still on his tongue as it swirled against hers, giving her gustatory as well somatosensory pleasure. Dexter made a sudden move and balanced a knee on each side of her hip, his manhood protruding toward the sky. "Do you want this?"

"Yes."

He reached for the wine bottle and gave it to her. Then, without a word, he lay down, stretched himself to his full six feet two inches (plus nine, but who's counting?) and closed his eyes. Faye was tentative. This was new ground. She'd performed oral sex once or twice, but that had been years ago and even then, if she recalled correctly, it had been forgettable at best. What if she disappointed him? After the way he'd rocked her world, she wanted to do no less than return the favor.

"I don't know how to please you that way," she admitted.

"Do what I did to you, baby. Wet me down with the wine, then dry me off with your tongue."

Faye poured wine on his shaft, swirled her tongue around his mushroom tip, tickled his sac, and then buried as much of his length as possible in her hot, wet mouth. Up and down, over and again she worshipped at his penile shrine. Dexter almost came right then.

"Get on and ride me, baby," he said in a whisper, his hips beginning the movement that he'd continue once inside. After one final kiss, Faye eased down on his piercing-hot girth, contracting and releasing her Kegel muscles and driving him wild. Heady with her newfound control, she once again rose to the tip of his goodness, and then slowly, oh…so…slowly, lowered herself until he was fully inside her. Placing her hands on his expansive chest, she began a rhythm that allowed Dexter to touch her very soul: back and forth, up and down, side to side, push, pull. With the sun going down and the wind kissing her bare skin, she felt total abandon, massaging her own breasts as she clasped her thighs and rode them both into ecstasy.

Afterward they lay there, in their own private Garden of Eden: naked, satiated and content. Faye nestled into the crook of Dexter's arm, watching the first star of the night begin to twinkle against the endless sky.

"I'm going to miss this place."

"This place," Dexter asked, positioning her closer, "or me?"

"You're not what I expected," she said again.

"Neither are you."

Faye turned her face toward him. "What did you think the first time you saw me?"

"When I saw you that first day, standing there in those raggedy clothes, I didn't know what to think." He dodged her punch. "What? You know you were looking tore down."

"It was a long trip."

"You could wear a paper bag and still look good." His gaze was intense, letting her know he meant it. "When you were standing at the edge of the patio, deciding whether or not to go in the party, I thought that you were shy, unsure of herself, probably an introvert who didn't socialize often."

"That's mostly true. I wouldn't say shy but definitely the more introverted, studious type."

"Then when Papa Dee collapsed, I saw a whole other woman. One who was confident and intelligent, totally capable of commanding a situation. The dichotomies intrigued me. I wanted to know more."

"That's why you asked me out?" Darkness continued to fall, yet she could feel Dexter nod beside her. "I've enjoyed my stay here, and you, but the truth is that we come from two very different worlds, and we're going in different directions. You are the heir to a very profitable enterprise known as Drake Wines Resort and Spa that caters to the wealthy, and I am getting ready to start up a free clinic, a center to serve the very poor. What I'm about to undertake is a challenging endeavor. There's a building to try and get renovated, staff to hire, volunteers to recruit. It will take up all of my time."

"You've already secured a place for your clinic?"

"Yes, but it needs work." Faye gave him the short version of the building purchased at a fraction of its value from a successful San Diego pastor: Jack Kirtz of Open Arms Ministry.

"My brother-in-law owns a construction company. I could talk to him about helping you."

"Really? Dexter, that would be wonderful. We're being very frugal with our budget but—"

"Don't worry about that." He kissed her forehead. "You can be one of our charitable contributions."

"Thanks. I think."

A moment of silence before Dexter spoke again. "There's a lot on my plate, too. I work very hard. But everyone needs a break from routine now and then, a chance to relax, reflect and take care of...personal needs."

"I'm sure you'll have no lack of women wanting to help you do that."

"True. But I'm not talking to them right now. I'm talking to you."

"We'll see," she said finally, wondering but not asking about the other women who were surely in Dexter's life; not wanting to know if there was one significant other or several, not wanting to care whether they existed or not. The truth of the matter was that all too soon she'd pack her things, check out of the hotel, head to San Diego and start her new life. She saw long days, hard work and much sacrifice ahead. And very little room for either relaxing or reflecting with a man named Dexter Drake.

Chapter 21

Faye's last night at Drake Wines Resort & Spa had been spent in Dexter's arms. During her time with him they'd ridden horses and she'd picked grapes, and they'd gathered and cooked greens out of Papa Dee's garden. She'd interviewed homecare nurses and chosen one for Papa Dee. Before leaving she and Dexter had exchanged cell phone numbers, and he'd promised to have his brother-in-law, Jackson Wright, call the following week about the clinic's renovation. Yet now, almost seventy-two hours later, her time at the resort and with Dexter seemed like a dream. There'd been so much to do since then: move into her rented condo, meet with Pastor Jack and the volunteers from his church, set up appointments to interview nurses and talk with San Diego State about the students she'd like to see later that week. The clinic was set to open in thirty days. Faye imagined she'd be a zombie by then.

Her cell phone rang and she was grateful for the interruption. "Hello?"

"Take a break, Doctor."

Her heart flip-flopped. "Hello, Dexter."

"You sound tired. Are you already buried in work?"

"Pretty much. I've managed to put together a semblance of an office here where the center will be located." She shared a bit of what she'd been doing for the past three days. "What about you? Making wine? Chasing women?"

"No, this week I'm wearing my business hat. Donovan and I are in Northern California, preparing to expand the Drake Wines brand."

"I didn't get to meet your brother."

"He's a workaholic. Something that it seems the two of you have in common." A pause and then, "So…I've been thinking about our time together, you know, holes and poles."

"Fishing, correct?"

"What else, baby?" Faye laughed. "When am I going to see you again?"

Faye's thighs clenched of their own volition. She'd had to continually force thoughts of Dexter out of her head to get any work done. It had been a constant struggle, and now the effort would begin anew. "You're very tempting, but honestly, I don't know. My schedule is jam-packed for the next few weeks. Oh, wait. I have an idea. How would you like to join me at our benefit fundraiser? The hoity-toity world is not much my scene but will be right up your alley—tuxedos, ball gowns and fancy food."

"Hoity-toity?" Dexter laughed. "You're a trip. When is it?"

"Next Saturday night." She gave him the details.

"With this new venture and the ongoing harvest, my schedule is a little crazy right now too. So no promises, but I'll definitely try and make it if I can."

Despite his tendency to distract her, Dexter's phone

call was the pick-me-up she needed. She waded through the rest of the résumés from professional nurses and made a good dent in narrowing down the student choices. Two additional agencies had also come through with small donations. Faye was grateful. Every little bit helped. Her last phone call was the perfect ending to her Monday. Dexter's brother-in-law, Jackson, the construction company owner who was married to Diamond, had agreed to come by tomorrow and take a look at the building. Depending on what he found upon inspection, he'd told her, the renovation could begin as early as Friday. It seemed Faye had waited a lifetime to see her dream of a free clinic turned into reality. She couldn't wait.

She stopped by the store and after a light dinner of soup and salad, Faye climbed into her queen-size bed with a folder of possible additional donors for the clinic. There were governmental agencies, private agencies, individuals and grant possibilities. The work was overwhelming. Doctor Ian had provided the initial assistance and financial support but his hands were full with Haitian Heartbeats. Faye needed local help. A vision worth doing was not one that could be done alone. For the umpteenth time since this journey began, she thought about Gerald McPherson. Back in Africa, they'd worked so well together. At one time, starting a clinic had also been his dream. But then he had to up and fall in love, get married and fall off the face of the planet. *No, that's not entirely true,* Faye thought, picking up another résumé. She read somewhere a year or so ago that he was practicing at a hospital in Baltimore.

Her phone vibrated. This time, unlike before, she looked at the caller ID before answering. "Addie! I left a message for you days ago. Where have you been?"

"Faye, forgive me. I meant to call. But the hubby surprised me with a weekend getaway. The kids stayed with his parents. We flew to Barbados."

"Ah, that sounds so romantic. I know you guys love your babies, but sometimes it's good to have grown-up time."

"Yes, it was good all right. So good that in nine months, I think we might have another mouth to feed."

"Ha!"

"So what's going on, girl?"

Faye filled her in on the whirlwind otherwise known as Dexter. "It was good to have my head on straight going in. Neither one of us is looking for anything permanent. I'm too busy and he's too wild."

"Life's too short to worry about the future. I'm just happy to hear that you're finally living, really *living,* in the here and now."

"Look, can I call you back in a couple of hours? I have to finish going through these résumés. My first appointments are tomorrow."

"I thought the building needed fixing?"

"It does, and that's the other thing. Dexter's brother-in-law owns a construction company. He's agreed to do the work."

"Hmm, sounds like this Dexter guy is quite the catch. Are you sure he's not what you're looking for?"

"On that note, let me call you back so that we can finish catching up."

"I can do you one better than that."

"Really? What?"

"I can come there and attend your fancy fundraiser, maybe get a look at the man who brought you back to life."

Faye whooped. "Oh, please try and come, Addie. Having you here would mean everything. We would have a blast!"

"Okay. I'll call you later with my flight information.

In the meantime, make sure that your man will be in attendance. I have to check him out and give my blessing."

"He said he'd make it if he could. And he isn't my man."

"He may not be your man for permanent, but it sounds like he's the one for temporary."

Chapter 22

"Hey, Corey! What's happening?" The week had been crammed with non-stop work, and Dexter was more than ready to chill. He hadn't heard from his college roommate and best friend for months. It was just the type of diversion he needed to break from the business at hand. "I see that marriage has a brother on lockdown. How many minutes are you allowed on the phone?"

"Whatever," Corey Foster said above Dexter's laughter. "You know me well enough to know I rule the roost."

"I'm just messing with you, dog. Where are you?"

"On your side of the world."

"Word? You're in L.A.?"

"Close—San Francisco."

"That's even better!" Dexter explained to Corey that he too was in Northern California and why.

"Jermaine and Mike are here, too."

"What is this? An impromptu reunion?" These four had

met during a summer sports camp. Through different high schools, colleges and relocations, they'd remained close until recent years when marriage and starting families had interrupted their semi-annual meetings.

"Of sorts. Jermaine accepted another job. He's working with the Raiders franchise now."

"The Raiders? You know I'm a Chargers man."

"Don't matter. He's hooked us up for the weekend—hot, private party with some of Oakland's finest, presidential suite on Saturday night and seats in the owner's box on Sunday for the preseason game. Don't even think about not showing up. It's been too long. We all need to reconnect."

"Hey, I'll be there—don't trip about that. This week has been grueling. Hanging out with you fools is just what I need."

"Tell me where you're at so we can send a limo."

"Oh, Jermaine's got it like that?"

"Yeah, bro. It's like that."

Dexter hung up the phone and double-checked his electronic calendar. There was a niggling feeling that he was forgetting something that was happening, but he always put everything he even thought about doing in his phone. So he dismissed the temporary uneasiness and got ready to spend the weekend with his boys.

In San Diego, Faye was in a wonderful mood, delighted to have her best friend visiting California. She and Adeline had been gabbing nonstop since meeting at the airport, catching up over a quick lunch at the scenic Seaport Village located just moments from the airport and continuing their spirited conversation during the mini-tour Faye had given Adeline around her neighborhood. Now, as they prepared for the night's festivities, the two con-

tinued the easy camaraderie that had been a trademark of
their friendship from day one.

"You look good, girl." Adeline looked at her friend with
true admiration. "Who knew that you'd clean up so well?"

"Forget you, Addie. This isn't the first time you've seen
me dressed up."

"If you're talking about that black dress that you used
to pull out for every dinner, then I beg to differ."

The women laughed as Faye rechecked her image in
the mirror. She was wearing a fuchsia-colored designer
original, or so that's what the woman who donated the
dress told her. A stylist had done her hair and makeup.
She hadn't looked this pretty since Drake Wines Resort
and Spa and Papa Dee's party.

Dexter. For a moment, Faye's happiness faltered, but
she quickly recovered. He said he'd try and come to the
benefit. He hadn't promised he would. The week had been
so crazy and she'd been so busy that honestly, she hadn't
given her invitation to have him join her at the benefit a
second thought. Until today and Adeline's arrival. "When
will I meet him?" had been asked almost before "How are
you?" Faye refused to call him. The last thing she wanted
to come off as was a woman with expectations. There had
been no illusions about what she and Dexter shared. If he
showed up, fine. If not, she'd stay focused on the reason
for the evening. The money Dr. Ian provided wouldn't last
forever. They were raising money to ensure the future of
the Heart of Healing Center.

"So why are you trying to be all secretive, girl? Will
I get to meet your man tonight?" Adeline asked as they
headed to the chauffeured car that a donor had provided.

"Maybe," was Faye's noncommittal answer.

They arrived at the event and almost as soon as Faye
entered the room she was whisked away by her PR con-

sultant to meet first this person and then the next. As the daughter of one of Haiti's most prominent citizens before his death, Adeline was in her element and had no problem introducing herself to those she encountered, and making polite conversation with San Diego's elite. Faye wasn't as comfortable being front and center but she plastered on a bright smile and braved the media and high-profile potential donors. All of the hoopla was almost enough to make her forget that she'd invited Dexter to the event. Almost.

But the fact that her eyes kept scanning the room and glancing toward the door wasn't missed by Adeline. "I'm sure there's a good reason he's not here," she offered, when the two had a private moment.

"It doesn't matter," Faye said with a shrug.

But both of them knew that it did.

Dexter knew he was in for a night of madness. He'd met his friends at the upscale hotel where they'd be staying. They'd changed clothes and now found themselves in a mansion located in the Blackhawk area east of Oakland, surrounded by good food, great drink and beautiful women. Corey, who was married and faithful, had found himself a spot near the pool and was engaged in a serious game of chess. Jermaine and Mike had disappeared shortly after being greeted by the host. Dexter sampled a glass of bubbly from the roaming waiter as he admired the modern architecture of the mansion's design.

"Hey, handsome!" a sultry voice purred.

Dexter turned and saw a vision. "Well, hello."

She was all breasts and legs and long, black hair. A weave probably, but it hardly mattered. Her skin was darkly tanned and flawless, the come-hither red of her lips a perfect match with long manicured nails. Looking at this dose of loveliness reminded Dexter that a week of research and business meetings had left him no time for sex. And the last time he had a good dose of that was... *damn! The benefit!* Dexter immediately reached for his phone. He checked missed calls and messages. None from Faye. There was a twinge of disappointment quickly replaced by relief. She hadn't called. Not once. He hadn't heard from her all week. Obviously she didn't need him. If she'd really wanted him to accompany her to the "hoity-toity" function she'd mentioned, she would have called with more details. He was chagrinned, but still made a mental note to send her a text later.

"How are you, beautiful?"

"Better now." Beautiful slithered up against him. "What's your name, handsome?"

"Dexter. What's yours?"

"Taylor."

"Nice to meet you, Taylor."

"Likewise. I love that watch. A Rolex, right?"

Okay, here we go. Trying to figure out the bank account. He nodded. "You know your brands."

She tossed the thick mane of silky hair over her shoulder. "I know quality when I see it." She gave him the once-over. "What do you do?"

"I help to run a business," was his noncommittal reply.

The conversation went on in a similar vein not only with Taylor, but others. They weren't all golddiggers; maybe none of them was. But their polished looks, red-bottom pumps, diamonds and ample cleavage didn't move him in the way it usually did. For some crazy reason he kept thinking of Faye: the fishing and cooking and times spent with Papa Dee. He flitted and flirted and had a good time, but only a couple of hours into the evening he found Corey, told him that he'd see him tomorrow before the game, and had the driver take him back to the hotel.

He reached the room and idly turned on the television, flipping through the channels and settling on a cable news show. He undressed and went to the bathroom. When he returned to the living room, the woman who'd never been far from his thoughts was on the screen. It was Faye, looking svelte and elegant in a bright-colored gown that molded to her lanky figure and highlighted her dark skin. She stood poised and confident, and in that moment Dexter was reminded of his mother. He turned up the volume and listened as she talked about the center and how much it was needed in San Diego and the surrounding communities. She thanked those who'd given and graciously asked for more support. Dexter watched and was deeply moved as he saw her truly in her element; moved by the videos taken from her time in Haiti, and from the low- or no-income parents now hopeful for healthcare. While sending her a text, he also vowed to write a check and plan a trip to San Diego.

He wasn't the only one watching and wasn't the only one planning to pay a visit to Dr. Buckner very soon.

Chapter 23

Faye was pleased that everything regarding the center was coming together, its imminent opening still felt like a dream. The benefit fundraiser had been very successful and it had been wonderful spending time stateside with Adeline. Dexter had sent a text; his apology made more palatable with the news that his brother-in-law was beginning construction the following week. Rather than reveal how much his no-show had hurt her, she'd responded nonchalantly, acting like it was no big deal. She was grateful for the construction work that due to Dexter's involvement was being donated. Even now as she sat in the hotel conference room that served as her temporary office, Boss Construction was turning the building that had been donated into a wonderful clinic with a waiting room, patient rooms, offices and more. Faye had hired a wonderful young woman she'd met through Open Arms. Vickie was a godsend, answering phones, checking emails and handling other administrative duties, allowing Faye to focus on PR and staff. On this Monday after the benefit, Faye had just returned to the conference room/office following a meeting with the newly appointed board, when Vickie handed her a stack of messages. She walked to the other side of the conference room, where a second phone was located. Halfway there she stopped, did a double-take at the piece of paper she was holding and let out a yelp.

"What is it, Dr. Buckner?" Vickie asked, concern in her voice.

"Sorry, Vickie. That was a sound of surprise and delight. This Gerald McPherson who left a message is a fellow doctor and old friend whom I haven't seen in several years." She hurried to the phone, dialed the number and, after announcing herself to the receptionist, sat back and waited to hear a booming voice.

He didn't disappoint. "Buck!"

"Fear!"

The use of each other's nicknames immediately made it feel as though no time had passed. "I couldn't believe it when I saw your name! How did you find me?"

"I saw you on television the night of your benefit and I was bowled over. Listening to you took me right back to those times when we shared our dreams. You did it, Buck," he continued, his voice softening with affection. "You wanted to run a free clinic in America…and it's happening."

"Pretty amazing, isn't it?" Faye exclaimed. "What about you, Gerald? The last I heard you were practicing in Baltimore. Are you still at that hospital? And how is married life treating you? Do you have children? There is so much I've wondered about over the years. It's so good to talk to you!"

"I feel the same. My life, the short version? I'm still working at a public hospital and have a beautiful daughter, Rene, who's three. But her mother and I didn't work out. My divorce was final six months ago."

"Gerald, I'm sorry."

"Don't be. In reconnecting with my high school sweetheart, I married a memory. Once we were under one roof, it became clear that we'd grown into two very different people. We're still cordial for the sake of our child." A pause and then, "What about you, Buck? Are you still single or one of those liberated women determined to keep your maiden name?"

"I'm married to my career." She gave a brief recount of her remaining years in Africa and the time she'd spent in Haiti before returning stateside.

"And here you are, about to dive headfirst into another challenging situation that will test your whole skill set and take all your time."

"I'm still the workaholic you remember."

There was a companionable moment of silence before Gerald spoke again. "It's good to talk to you, Faye. I've never forgotten you in all these years."

"There's no forgetting those special times in Africa. Our team was unique."

"We did a lot of good there. I still miss it sometimes."

"I could use a good doctor here in San Diego." The words were out before Faye could truly contemplate their meaning.

"Sounds like an offer, Buck. I'll give it serious consideration."

"Please do. Eventually we'd like to duplicate this model in cities across the country. The board will be looking for someone to head that up. I think you'd be perfect." They spoke a few more minutes and exchanged cell phone numbers. Faye thought she'd gotten the surprise of the day.

Then Dexter walked through the door.

"Dexter!" A sight for sore eyes didn't begin to explain his appearance.

"Hello, Doctor." The greeting was casual, the fire burning in his eyes…anything but.

His sexy smile melted away the last vestiges of disappointment at him forgetting about attending the benefit.

"This is a pleasant surprise," she said. "Especially since I'm not at the facility."

"I talked to Jackson. He informed me of these temporary offices. I'd rather have learned that from you, but since a brother hasn't gotten a phone call…" He smiled to show he was teasing, and then looked over at Vickie—who was staring unabashedly—and winked.

"Since leaving the resort my life's been a whirlwind— even more so than I imagined it would be. Sorry I haven't kept in touch."

"No worries. Apology accepted. I've been busy, as well."

Faye stood. "Vickie, I'm going to step out for a minute. If Pastor Jack or the college calls, please let both of them know that I'll return the call shortly." They left the conference room and headed toward a bar area located in the hotel lobby. "How's Papa Dee?"

"Getting stronger every day—and still asking about you."

"I hope I haven't upset him. I promised to call."

"So you're a woman who doesn't keep her promises?"

"I am a woman of my word. I didn't say exactly when I'd call him…"

"Ha! Way to wiggle out of that one, Faye."

"But I do feel bad. I'll call him tonight."

"What about me?" Dexter asked, once they'd reached the bar and chosen a booth in the back. "What are you going to do to make up for ignoring me?"

"Uh, I believe I'm the one who was stood up at her gala."

"Baby, how many times do I have to apologize about that? And you still didn't call me, even after I sent the text apologizing *and* set things in motion to get the construction started on your clinic."

"I sent a text back thanking you; just like you texted me."

"You should have called." Dexter didn't care that he was pouting like he was two. He wasn't used to being ignored.

His attitude was endearing and Faye's heart skipped a beat as she noted the scowl. "Is someone feeling neglected?"

He reached across the table and began to stroke Faye's hand. "More like some*thing*."

"Oh." Faye felt herself flush from her toes to her ears. *Does this mean that he hasn't been with anyone since our tryst last week?* The possibility surprised her, and made her smile. She would never admit knowing Dexter had been intimate with another woman would bother her...but it would. Even more of a bother was how at the memory of past intimacies every nerve ending in her va-jay-jay was now throbbing with need. Time to change the subject. Fast.

"Thank you so much for setting me up with your brother-in-law for the clinic's renovation. He thinks the crew can be finished in two weeks. That's amazing."

"Jackson knows his stuff. They've already handled most of the electrical work and the flooring. Now they're putting up the framing so that tomorrow they can start on the walls."

"How do you know so much about what's happening at my clinic?"

"I've got it like that," he drawled, his twinkling eyes

framed by those ridiculously long lashes while his mouth was fixed in that impish grin she'd come to love.

"Is that so?"

"Isn't it?"

Faye couldn't lie. It was. Yet she decided not to stroke his healthy ego. Especially when she'd much rather stroke something else.

"You probably assumed that I talked to Jackson on the phone, but I actually stopped by the building. He showed me what they've been able to do thanks to using a double crew."

Faye eyed Dexter with a look of appreciation. If she were into having a relationship, she could really come to like this guy. "What has you in San Diego? I know you didn't drive down just to see me."

Dexter didn't dispel the assumption Faye had made. He was too busy hiding behind the excuse he'd given himself for his trip down the I-15. "My brother lives down here. Donovan and his wife, Marissa."

"I see."

"I saw you on television the other night. It looks like your benefit was a success."

"Yes."

"I wish you'd call to give me the details about the affair. That would have served as a reminder."

"You were waiting for me?" Faye was genuinely surprised. And a little miffed. "I gave the verbal invitation. If you were serious about going, then you should have called me."

"Straight-shooting Faye Buckner. You know I like that about you."

"Well?" She crossed her arms. "I wasn't going to bring it up but...why didn't you attend the benefit?"

"Honestly, I forgot." Faye huffed. "I know," Dexter continued, putting up his hands in defense. "And I'm sorry. It's rare that I don't record something in my phone, but somehow your fundraiser didn't make it in." He told her about hearing from his longtime friends. "I want to make it up to you."

"How so?"

"For starters, with this." He reached into his jacket pocket, pulled out a check and slid it across the table.

Faye's eyes widened. She looked from Dexter to the check and back to Dexter again. "Fifty thousand dollars? This is too generous. I…I don't know what to say."

"Thank you works."

"Those two words hardly seem adequate, but thank you, seriously, from the bottom of my heart."

"No worries. My family is more than happy to help."

Again, Faye was assailed with a myriad of emotions that she didn't want to acknowledge, let alone handle. So again, she steered the conversation to what she hoped were safer grounds. "Did you have a good time with your friends in Oakland?"

He shrugged. "It was all right. I would have had a better time with you."

Faye somewhat relaxed. "You are such a flirt!"

"Only when I'm around pretty women with whom I'm envisioning, uh, intercourse." Faye looked away, embarrassed and turned on at the same time. "So what about it, Doctor? Let's say you give me a tour of your new place, help me get acquainted with your bedroom, and I'll help reacquaint you to something you like."

Chapter 24

Two hours later, Dexter pulled up to a small, well-maintained condominium complex that was tucked away on a quaint block lined with tall trees on the manicured lawns of single-family homes. While Faye had finished up the time-sensitive projects on her desk, he'd used his spare key to hang out at Donovan's house and handle some family business by phone. Maintaining his focus hadn't been easy. He hadn't been this turned on by the thoughts of seeing a woman in a long time.

"This looks like you," he commented once Faye had answered the door. "Earthy, straightforward, practical, no-nonsense."

"Guess I never was the flowery, frilly kind of girl."

He turned and saw a painting anchoring the far wall. It was of a magnificent sunset, with the red, yellow and orange emphasized. "But in the midst of all the order burns a fire." Those words changed the atmosphere in an instant. "Come. Here."

She could do no other than comply. Within seconds she was in his arms, with hands groping and tongues twirling and fingers fumbling for buttons to get undone. "Let's go to the bedroom," Faye whispered against his mouth, even as the blouse that she'd almost torn off was thrown on the floor.

"I want you right here, right now."

Faye had been giving orders for the past three days. Who was she to argue?

He turned her around, pulled the skirt she wore over her narrow hips while admiring the round booty that fit perfectly in his hands, kissed the dimples that rested just above her mounds and slid a finger along its crease.

"Ooh."

"Did you miss me?" Dexter's voice was soft, raspy, as he rubbed himself against her.

"Yes," she whispered, feeling him harden and lengthen against her.

He guided her hands to the couch's arm. Bending that way left her exposed. Just the way Dexter liked it. His fingers played a familiar melody against her furry fortress, preparing her to receive his super-sized shaft. It didn't take long. She jiggled her butt against him, her body begging for what he'd come to give. He slid on protection and then slid inside her—slowly, methodically—inch by delicious inch. Faye relaxed and exhaled, the rhythm between them coming naturally. He reached around for her small yet pert breasts, tweaked the nipples into the pebbled hardness he remembered. She moaned, clutching him with her inner muscles, moving her body like a belly dancer, balancing herself on the wedges she still wore. When she reached behind her to tickle his fancy, he could no longer hold back. He grabbed her hips, his mouth a firm line of concentration as he thrust himself in to the hilt, over and again, stenciling his name on her soul. He heard her began to pant, felt the soft quivers that preceded her moment of joy.

But it wasn't okay that she'd been able to leave the resort and go on with life as though she'd never been with "The Dexter." No other woman had been able to walk away, even for a few days, without reassurance that there would be more love. How dare she act as though she could live without him? No, he wanted to take her even higher. He wanted to leave her feening, like a junkie for a needle. He wanted to become her bad habit. So rather than take her over the edge this very second he stopped, pulling her up to kiss her back and shoulders before turning her around to plunder her mouth. Prolonging her pleasurable pain, he massaged her shoulders while he nibbled her earlobes and blew air on her neck. Before she could think, he eased her down on the couch, gliding his tongue down her body, nibbling her inner thighs and teasing her heat. He made love to her with his fingers and then with his tongue, hitting parts of Faye in ways that hadn't been covered in anatomy class. He hit her spot and it felt as though she shattered into a million pieces. She pulled him to her, welcomed his weight as he sheathed his sword inside her one final time and only now, when he was sure he'd given over and beyond the type of loving imagined, did he allow himself to let go, moaning her name as he shivered.

Later, Dexter and Faye lay amid her crumpled bedding, courtesy of another frenzied round of making love. They munched on grapes, cheese and crackers, drank Perrier and easily bounced from one topic to another.

"Have you ever been to a third world country," Faye asked.

"No."

"Would you be open to visiting one?"

"Where...like Haiti?"

"Haiti is the poorest country on the Western Hemisphere. It would be a good place to start."

"I don't have to actually visit a place to provide assistance, or show compassion. I appreciate helping the less fortunate, but hands-on interaction isn't me."

"I know. And I'm not judging."

"Sometimes it sounds like it."

"Really, I'm not. The only reason I bring it up is because of how seeing true poverty up close changes lives. Citizens of rich countries often take what they have for granted. In the few days I've been back, I've listened to kids whom I want to spank and then put in time-out. The words coming out of their mouths, the sense of entitlement…so different from the little ones who've grown up responsible for making sure the family has clean water or helping the mother pick vegetables from the garden or watch their younger siblings. I'm going back there in a few months and—" she shrugged"—never mind. It was a crazy idea."

Dexter rose up on an elbow and looked at Faye. "You're going back to Haiti and you want me to go with you?" She nodded. "Well, why didn't you just ask me? Be direct, the way you were when you wanted sexual intercourse." A quick kiss softened the chiding tone.

"Will I ever live down my loose tongue during a moment of inebriation?"

"Probably not."

"Whatever."

A companionable silence ensued for a moment. "I'll go," he said at last.

"You will?"

"Don't sound so astonished."

"You will!"

"Okay, now you're being sarcastic."

Faye rolled over and straddled Dexter, slowly grinding

her hips as she showered him with kisses. "I must admit there are perks to your lifestyle," she breathed, her voice husky, his sex already responding.

"Like what?"

"Your car. Um. I like it."

Dexter's smile widened at the mention of his baby. "Well, all right woman," he murmured, easing himself inside her. "Let's get ready to ride!"

Chapter 25

The week passed quickly. Faye not only called Papa Dee but promised to visit him the following Sunday. Her mountainous to-do list was slowly going down. The renovation was buzzing right along, and she'd hired a head nurse and selected four nursing students and received another donation from one of the county's elite. Plus she'd be seeing Dexter again. Life was good. She'd sent Vickie home at five o'clock and was preparing to leave herself when the phone rang.

"Hearts of Health and Healing Center, Dr. Buckner speaking."

"Buck!"

She smiled, set her purse on the desk and eased into the chair. "Fear. How are you?"

"I'm good, Faye. Real good. So how are your plans coming to save the world?"

"Ha! Working on it. And speaking of, have you had a chance to review the materials I sent you?"

"I did. That's why I'm calling. You've done great work, Faye. Looks like you've grown quite a bit over the years. Both as a doctor…and as a woman."

"Thank you." Faye answered casually, but her ears perked up. *Is he flirting with me?* At one time she'd had a huge crush on Gerald and had fantasized about the possibility of Dr. and Dr. McPherson. He was a brilliant doctor and an older man—ten years her senior. Unfortunately, he'd treated her more like a little sister than a romantic interest. Before she could get up the nerve to act on her feelings, he'd announced the engagement to his high school sweetheart and left the African jungle for an American city. "So are you calling to tell me that you've resigned your position in Baltimore and are ready to partner with me at this clinic?"

"I haven't gotten quite that far in the thought process, but you do present an interesting proposition. Like you, my heart is to help people, especially those less fortunate. I remember those nights when we'd sit under the stars and talk about doing this very thing. There's something very attractive about bringing those words to life. I have several things to consider, not the least of which would be an extensive pay cut. With child support and college funds, the finances are a huge concern," he said.

"That's why I'm working to find an attorney who's also well versed in grant-writing," Faye informed him. "My benefactor gave me enough to get started and run the clinic for a while. But hopefully we'd be able to fund your salary in five-year increments through grants, donations and other creative endeavors. With the increased visibility of marketing this model to urban communities nationwide, the possibility for speaking engagements would increase, not to mention your managing that whole area of operations once the workload demands." When he didn't immediately respond, she added, "Besides, wouldn't it be great to work together again?"

"Those were good years in Africa," Gerald admitted. "And building something from the ground up brings its own unique brand of satisfaction. I'll give the offer serious consideration, Faye."

"While you're thinking about it, why don't you make plans to attend the open house celebration, scheduled for the first Saturday in October? I'd love to introduce you to the board, the staff that has been hired to date and Pastor Jack Kirtz, the man whose ministry has been so helpful in getting the clinic off the ground."

"Let's see, the first weekend…" She could hear papers being shuffled. "It looks open right now. I'll double-check and confirm next week. How does that sound?"

"Wonderful, Gerald. It would be great to see you."

"You, too."

Faye was a bit apprehensive as she pulled up to the Drake estate. At first she hadn't hesitated about joining Dexter and his family for Sunday dinner, but now she wasn't so sure it had been a good idea. True, she adored Papa Dee, had felt comfortable during her brief exchange with Diamond, and believed the rest of them all to be good people, but she hadn't seen any of them since she and Dexter had become intimate. It had been awhile since she'd had a man, even longer since she'd had to interact with his family. How much did they know of her and Dexter's friendship? He'd admitted that theirs was a very close-knit family. How much of his personal life did Dexter share?

Only one way to find out, she thought, exiting the car and smoothing her hand over the beige-colored silk top that she'd paired with dark brown slacks. Flat sandals, hoop earrings and minimum makeup completed the look.

She walked up the steps and crossed the porch. The door opened before she could grab the knocker.

"Dr. Buckner!" Genevieve exclaimed, with arms wide. She enveloped Faye in a gentle embrace. "It's so good to see you again. Come on in. Everyone's inside."

Ten minutes into their boisterous sit-down dinner and Faye knew that her previous worries had been for naught. The conversation flowed as easily as the wine as sibling and in-law vied for center stage. Faye took it all in with bright eyes and a smile. For years it had mostly been her and her mother, except for the brief times her dad had been home on leave. Later, when her mother remarried, Faye continued to spend great amounts of time alone. Her half-brother was a baby who demanded attention, and as he grew older so did his presence in the house. Richard was more like their mother, and her stepfather was delighted to finally have a son. Faye often felt like an afterthought, invisible, and while her mother often recognized her intellectual abilities and complimented her on her good grades, Faye felt they never totally related to each other. Going away for college was almost a relief.

"Are you all right?" Genevieve asked Faye, during a break in the melee. "Would you like more jambalaya, or garlic bread?"

"I'm stuffed, but it's delicious," Faye said, and then added, "Okay, maybe just a little bit more of the jambalaya."

"Now that's what we like to hear! Dexter, can you dish your lady, I mean, the doctor, up another helping?"

Donovan chuckled. Dexter snorted. Diamond hid her laugh behind a cough.

"Don't mind my wife, Dr. Buckner," Donald said with a voice as calm as a desert breeze. "She means well but often confuses other people's business with her own."

"Well, now, that *is* his lady," Papa Dee piped in. "Least that's what it looked like when I caught them in the kitchen making whoopee instead of spaghetti."

A cacophony of voices ensued with rebuttals, questions and comments being tossed around in equal proportion. Being embarrassed was pointless, so instead she sat back, enjoyed the best Creole cuisine she'd ever eaten and watched the Drake show. Rather the common consensus be that she was Dexter's lady instead of the sexy freak she planned on becoming later that night when they were alone. If Papa Dee got a glimpse at *that* impending love scene, the conversation would go to a whole other level!

Later that night, the lovemaking between her and Dexter was sweeter than the pound cake Miss Mary had made, just as Faye had imagined.

Chapter 26

"Can you believe it, Dr. Buckner?" Vickie exclaimed. "Can you believe this day has finally arrived?"

"No, Vickie, I can't. As the program unfolds, I may ask you to pinch me to make sure I'm not dreaming."

"This is no dream, Dr. Buckner. Just the results of hard work and faith."

Perhaps, but it seemed a miracle nonetheless, such as a week ago, when she'd walked through the newly renovated center, or the days following that when truckloads of furniture, medical equipment, beds and the like transformed the empty building into a place ready to treat illnesses and encourage healthy lifestyles. She'd loved Pastor Jack's suggestion to lessen the storage space and set up a small exercise classroom for community residents, where aerobics and nutrition could be taught. A local fitness center had heard of their desire and donated equipment. To see the gleaming stationary bicycles, treadmills and elliptical machines were more than she'd ever imagined, and the tables and chairs of her "classroom" were beyond all she dared hope. It would have been great if Dr. Ian and Adeline had been able to come for the opening, but she understood they were needed where they were. And while the huge bouquet of flowers was lovely, she'd so looked forward to seeing her old friend Gerald McPherson. He'd sent the flowers and his regrets, promising to phone her next week. And finally there were the Drakes. That family was really something else. She'd insisted it wasn't necessary, but all of them—save Papa Dee and Dexter's grandparents, Mary and David Sr.—had promised to attend her big day. She'd spoken to Dexter and expected them to arrive around two-thirty, just before the three o'clock ribbon cutting. It was going to be a very big day.

"Have we checked with the nurses about the blood pressure and diabetes monitors?"

"All set, Doctor. Also, the extra volunteers who will be used to do those screenings should be arriving within the hour."

"Good. What about the appointment applications for next week's adult and child physicals?"

"I ran off a hundred more copies, just to be sure. My mom also came by to help me tweak the filing system so everything is alphabetized right away."

"You're a godsend, Vickie."

She smiled. "I try." They heard bells jingling, the sign that the door was being opened. "That's probably the caterers. I'll show them where to set up."

"Good deal." Faye looked at her watch. It was just before noon. She'd eaten nothing and should be starving but doubted anything could get past the nerves in her throat. She picked up her to-do list, checking and rechecking all of the particulars. The mayor's office had phoned confirming that he'd be there with a proclamation. Several community and church leaders would also be on hand, as would all of the donors and agencies that'd lent their support. The children's choir from Pastor Jack's church would sing the national anthem before the ribbon was cut.

Just relax, Faye told herself, feeling a stress headache trying to creep up on her. She walked to her desk, sat down, closed her eyes and practiced deep breathing. *In, hold it. One. Two. Three. And exhale. One. Two. Three.* Twice more, and Faye felt herself begin to relax. She rolled her head around to remove the kinks.

"I can handle that massage for you."

Faye's eyes flew open. Her mouth dropped. She sat there stunned.

"What, you don't have a hello and a hug for an old friend?"

Over her shock, Faye leaped from her chair and ran around her desk. "Gerald McPherson!" He pulled her into a bear hug, and they rocked back and forth. "You rascal. The flowers, and phone call saying you couldn't make it…"

"Yeah, well, I thought it would work better as a surprise."

She pulled back. "Let me look at you." She placed a hand on his cheek. "Okay, a little more crow's feet around the eyes—"

"Watch it, now."

"And, hmm…" Faye looked down. "Maybe another inch or two around the midsection…"

"Doctor…"

"Ha! I'm just teasing you, Fear, and it serves you right. I can't believe you're here!" She threw her arms around him for another big hug.

This was the scene that greeted Dexter when he turned the corner and walked through her opened door.

Chapter 27

Dexter stopped, his astute mind picking up everything in an instant: the joy in her voice, the prolonged embrace and the flowers he held that paled in comparison with the enormous bouquet sitting on the office credenza.

Who the hell is this?

Time to find out. But not before using the bouquet now seen as paltry to brighten up the receptionist desk. No way Dexter Drake would come in as number two. In anything. Cool as a cucumber, he returned to Faye's office and walked over to the couple, their backs to him, standing arm in arm. "Excuse me."

Faye's reaction was immediate, quickly stepping back from her good old friend. "Dexter, you're early!"

"Hey, baby." Dexter kissed Faye on the lips as he hugged her lightly, knowing his scent always drove her wild. He also knew that the khaki pants and discount-store shirt and tie that the chump beside her wore was no match for his tailored black Armani paired with his custom-designed, understated platinum bling. Dexter wasn't worried about competition. In his mind, he had none.

But just to be sure, he took the offensive. "Is this your relative, babe?" he said as he broke the embrace. He turned to Gerald and held out his hand. "Dexter Drake."

"*Dr.* Gerald McPherson," he brusquely responded.

"Gerald and I worked together in Africa," Faye hurriedly added.

"She's asked me to join her here," Gerald said, his smile smug and accommodating. He looked at Faye with admiring eyes. "Wanted me to be here for her big day; wants me to help her run this place." He turned back to Dexter. "We make a good team."

"Nothing like having someone capable working beside you." Dexter's reply was as smooth as silk as he kept his hand around Faye's waist. "The more she can employ your skills, the more time she can spend with me." His kiss on her temple underscored the point. "Good work, baby."

Vickie entered the office and Faye could have kissed her. "Sorry to interrupt, Doctor. But a couple of news trucks are here and want to know where to set up."

Faye didn't even think about inquiring as to the publicist's whereabouts. She made a beeline for Vickie and the office door. She didn't say anything. Just walked out.

Dexter moved to Faye's desk and sat down behind it, quickly making the unspoken statement that this was familiar territory and he felt totally comfortable in it. He pulled out his phone and began checking emails and texting.

Gerald, on the other hand, was visibly flustered. He'd been blindsided by Dexter's arrival and the pretty boy's obvious familiarity with the doctor. In hindsight it was naive to arrive unannounced, but he'd never considered

Faye would have a boyfriend. In all the time he'd known her that had never been the case. *Who was the guy she talked about, the one who left her shortly before I arrived in Africa?* The name was fuzzy, but the memory of Faye's position on dating when he arrived was clear. She wasn't interested. At least that's what he'd thought. He'd been somewhat attracted to her, even more so after seeing her skill and dedication, but having suffered a broken heart or two himself, he was in no mood to be rejected. He'd found it better to develop a professional camaraderie, treating her more like a sister or a best friend.

Deciding on a course of civility, Gerald walked over to Faye's desk and sat down in one of two leather chairs that faced it. "Detrick?"

A skeptical look and then, "Dexter."

"Right. How do you know Faye?"

"Isn't it obvious?" he said with a smirk.

"Not at all."

Now it was Dexter's turn to pause. From the beginning, both he and Faye had decided specifically not to title what they had as a relationship; no expectations, no particular rules. But if she wasn't his woman, or his girlfriend, then this Gerald joker would think that he had a chance. On the other hand, if he told Gerald that he and Faye were an item, a couple, then later on he might have some explaining to do. It was a tenuous situation at best. Dexter rarely gambled, but he was known as the poker king for a reason. One could never read his face or know his hand. So rather than answering, Dexter returned to his texts.

"Are you a doctor?" Gerald, a successful man in his own right, was not used to being usurped or ignored.

"No," Dexter said, his voice low and dismissive. "But some say I'm a healer."

"So your specialty is alternative medicine."

"Yes—" Dexter looked Gerald directly in the eye "—particularly where problems exclusive to a woman's well-being are concerned."

"I spent six weeks studying in China. What are some of the modalities that you employ?"

Well, brother, you start with a chilled bottle of sparkling wine followed by a strong, skilled tongue...

"Excuse me, Dr. McPherson?" Gerald was relieved to look up and see Faye's assistant standing in the doorway. "Dr. Buckner has asked that I come and get you. There are some people she wants you to meet."

Gerald stood and looked down at Dexter. "Duty calls," he said, before strolling out of the office, shoulders squared, head high.

"Your duty, my booty," Dexter mumbled, not at all happy that it was Gerald and not him that Faye had requested. This little development was going to make for an interesting evening. But Dexter knew he was more than ready for the challenge. If this stranger thought he was going to waltz into town and encroach on Drake territory, he had no idea what he was up against. None at all.

Chapter 28

Faye was exhausted, and the successful grand opening had nothing to do with it. No, she was tired from trying to keep up with where Dexter and Gerald were at any given time and keeping them occupied in different corners of the boxing ring otherwise known as Hearts of Health and Healing Center. Nothing overt had happened, yet when they were in close proximity she felt the tension could be cut with a Q-tip. Or maybe it was her paranoia and over-active imagination. Had something happened in the room before she'd pulled out Gerald to meet a member of the board? Should she have any reason to think the two men could not or would not get along? Dexter seemed non-plussed, but she hadn't missed that devilish twinkle in his eye. Gerald seemed annoyed, yet when she'd asked how he was doing, he'd said "fine."

"Doctor." Dexter sidled up next to Faye and placed his hand precariously close to her backside. True, they were next to the wall and few if any could see it, but still. Now was not the time.

"Stop it," she hissed through a pasted-on smile. "You're starting trouble and you need to quit."

"Why?" A swaddling babe couldn't have sounded more innocent. "What'd I do?"

"I don't know. But I'm hoping you'll tell me later."

"So you do plan for me to spend the night. Good, because watching you in your professional element is turning me on."

Faye's response was interrupted by a gorgeous blonde walking toward them. She greeted Dexter with a kiss on the cheek. "Hey, Dex."

A slightly raised brow was Faye's only reaction.

Subtle, but Dexter was nothing if not perceptive. "Hello, Erin. Dr. Buckner, this is—"

"Erin Bridges," Faye finished. "Erin has been helpful in securing donations for the center from several large firms." *Oh, I'm Dr. Buckner now. This must be one of your women.* Faye told herself that she didn't care; yet she couldn't help but tick off the differences between her and the woman now possessively holding Dexter's arm. Namely that Erin looked as if she stepped off a runway and Faye looked like, well, a doctor.

"Small world," Dexter said, his demeanor as unflappable as the statue holding the lamp in Manhattan's harbor. "Erin and Jackson have served on several committees together," he explained to Faye. "When held in this area, we often find ourselves at the same functions."

Very good, Dexter. Smoothly delivered and not one bead of sweat. This must not be your first time at this kind of dance. "Well, someone is motioning for me to join them. I'll leave you two to catch up."

Dexter deftly positioned himself so that he could see

where Faye headed. *Over to her doctor pal, Gerald. Why am I not surprised?* Dexter was working so hard at trying to look as though he wasn't looking that he didn't hear a word that Erin said.

"Dexter? Are you even listening?" She followed his line of sight. Looked at Faye. Looked at Dexter. "I guess not."

"What?"

"She's hardly your type."

"How would you know?" Dexter was scowling and didn't care. This whole jealousy situation was new territory, and it was beginning to fray his nerves. He walked away from Erin without a backward glance and over to where Donovan and Marissa chatted with another couple. He'd been so preoccupied he'd hardly been aware that his family had arrived. "Where's Jackson?" he asked when he reached them, after speaking to the strangers who were Donovan's new neighbors.

"Diamond is having contractions," Marissa explained. "You might be an uncle before long."

"When was somebody going to tell me?" Dexter demanded.

The couple said quick goodbyes and scurried away.

"Let me go and get you some punch," Marissa said slowly, trying to read her brother-in-law's unusual mood.

Donovan was less coddling. "Best to bring the bowl back so he can stick his face in it. He's acting pretty hot under the collar, and we don't want to set off the fire alarm." Dexter glared at his brother, who calmly checked his manicured nails. "Does it have anything to do with the doctor all cozied up with that pompous-looking dude?"

Dexter's head whipped around before he could stop it, taking in a very respectable scene of Faye, Gerald and the student nurses talking. "Very funny," he said in a manner that suggested Donovan's comment was anything but.

His brother's face broke into a wide smile. Dexter wanted to punch him in it.

"Well, well. Looks like somebody's woman is getting attention from another man and that somebody doesn't like it. Who is he?"

"Gerald McPherson, a doctor Faye worked with over in Africa."

"Oh, so they go *way* back." The daggers Dexter shot Donovan could have drawn blood. "I'm messing with you, little brother. But seriously, you need to readjust that armor of indifference toward the doctor that you've tried to wear. The coat is slipping."

"I'm not worried, Don. Baby girl isn't going anywhere."

"Funny, it looks like she's headed toward the hallway with her African alum."

Dexter's turn was slower this time but still timely enough to see Faye and Gerald disappear around the corner.

"I'm out of here, brother," he said, holding up his fist to Donovan for a pound. "I'll see you at the office tomorrow."

"Are you sure you want to leave?"

"Positive."

Dexter walked out the door without looking back, reached his Maserati GranCabrio and slid inside. Cranking Tupac's "California Love," he floored the gas and weaved in and out of traffic as he headed toward the highway. His eyes were narrowed, his countenance grim. He took the ramp to Interstate 5, headed north. Two miles down the road and already he was rolling at a smooth eighty-five. He figured at this speed he could be in L.A. in just over an hour. Faye Buckner wasn't the only woman in the world. *Hell, women will knock each other over to get to me!* And then Papa Dee's voice floated into his ear. *You always want to pick somebody who can stoke your fire, son, someone*

*who'll get your willy working, make you want to run a
mile...in bare feet!*

Dexter sighed, eased off the gas and took the next exit
on his way back to San Diego. Many women wanted him,
but right now there was only one woman he wanted. And
when she arrived home later tonight, he'd be there to greet
her—and anybody else who dared darken her door.

Chapter 29

"Vickie, have you seen Dexter?" It was 8 p.m. and the last of the grand opening guests were finally leaving. All Faye could think of doing was taking off her rarely worn heels and soaking in a tub.

"He left a while ago," she replied.

"Oh, did he leave with his family?"

"I don't think so, but I'm not sure. I saw him talking to a couple who I believe are part of the Drake family. The next time I noticed they were here but he was gone."

"Okay. Thanks, Vickie. You've been a tremendous help today. We'll clean all of this up tomorrow. Go on home. I'll lock up."

"Are you sure?"

"Yes." Faye looked up as Gerald came around the corner. "Is that everyone?"

Gerald nodded. "We're the last three standing."

"It was a pleasure meeting you, Dr. McPherson," Vickie said. "Dr. Buckner, I'll see you tomorrow."

Gerald and Faye watched Vickie walk out. Before she reached the sidewalk, Gerald had slipped behind Faye and began massaging her shoulders. "It's time for you to relax, Doctor," he said, his voice low and soothing. "You're as tight as a drum."

Faye reached back and patted his hand before moving away. "You're absolutely right, Gerald. A long, hot bath is calling my name." She turned to face him. "Where are you staying?"

He gave her the name of the hotel.

"How long are you here?"

"I leave Monday morning."

"I was hoping you'd say that. I'd love to spend time with you. We have so much catching up to do. But tonight I'm beat."

"Sure you don't have enough energy for one glass of champagne? A celebratory toast to your great achievement?"

"A glass of champagne would have me asleep at the bar. I'll be much better after a good night's rest. Can I treat you to breakfast tomorrow?"

"Sure, and then we can spend the day together."

"You've got it." She stepped toward him. They hugged. "Thanks again for coming, Gerald. It was so great to have you here."

"I'm not sure your boyfriend liked it."

Faye knew that Gerald was fishing, but this girl who knew a thing or two about the sport didn't take the bait. "Did you rent a car or take a taxi here?"

"I took a taxi."

"Let's get locked up and I'll drop you back to your hotel."

"That's okay, Faye. I can take a cab."

"Nonsense. It's not that far. Let's go."

Faye turned the corner onto her quiet block and thought that what she saw was surely a figment of her imagination. That was not a black Maserati in front of her condo building. She'd thought about Dexter all the way home, had wondered where he went and whether or not to call him, and she'd definitely salivated at the thought of getting one of his massages. Had she hoped so hard that she was now hallucinating? She pulled up to the parking lot gate and watched her hallucination get out of the car and walk toward her. So she was not just seeing things. The Maserati was real. And so was the man. "Hey, you," she said once he'd opened the passenger door.

"It's about time you got home."

"I would have come home sooner had I known you were waiting for me. Why'd you leave, and why didn't you tell me?"

"You were busy. I didn't want to bother you."

"Do you want to park your car inside the gate?"

"I've got a great security system. It will be fine."

They reached Faye's condo. Barely inside the door and she was pulling off her shoes. "I'm very grateful that the center is open, but I am so glad that open house is over."

"Looks like everyone had a good time. Especially your doctor friend."

Faye had been taking off her earrings. She stopped in mid-motion. "Gerald?"

"You know he's digging on you, right?"

"Please," Faye said, walking into the bedroom and removing her clothes. "The only thing Gerald is digging for is information on the center."

"Why is he so interested?" Dexter leaned against the doorjamb.

"He's a very good doctor, one with whom I've discussed my vision for the center, that's why. Where are all these questions coming from?"

Dexter shrugged. "I just don't like him."

"Wait. Are you jealous?"

"No."

"Are you sure?"

"Yes."

"Upset?"

"Do I have anything to be upset about?"

"No."

"Okay."

"Good. Now that that's settled, what do I have to do for a tub scrub and massage?"

Dexter sorta smiled, sorta pouted. "Nothing except get naked."

"Ha! Deal."

Chapter 30

Because they'd planned to spend the day together, Faye and Gerald had decided to have breakfast in the hotel restaurant. She handed her keys to the valet and rushed into the restaurant. Thirty minutes late.

"I'm so sorry," she said when she reached Gerald, who was sitting at the table reading a *USA TODAY*. He stood and they exchanged a light hug. "I overslept."

She sat down. Gerald eyed her intently. "Looks like you didn't sleep enough."

Is it that obvious? Probably was. It seemed that from the moment he found out that she was meeting Gerald for breakfast Dexter made it his mission to treat her like his last meal. The man had been insatiable, even waking her at 4 a.m. for another round! But given the way he woke her up, Faye had decided, she'd miss a little sleep. "I guess I was a little wound up when I got home," she offered, studying the menu. "And then, because she'd asked me to do so no matter how late, I called my best friend, Adeline, who lives in Haiti."

"Tell me about Haiti."

And with that, the moment of discomfort ended and Gerald and Faye fell into the comfortable banter honed over years of friendship. The waiter came and took their orders. She talked about Dr. Ian and the Haitian Heartbeats program, and the endless hope and resiliency of the people. He shared his experiences working in a large, public hospital; the bureaucratic frustrations, the budget limitations and why he was seriously considering a career change—namely, her offer. "I ran the idea by my ex," he finished, "told her I might be moving."

"How was that news received?"

"About the way I'd imagined—less concern about my whereabouts and more about child support payments."

"Wouldn't it bother you to be away from your daughter?"

Gerald nodded. "My girl is my heart and my biggest consideration. But if I am going to be away from her, now's the time. She's young enough that my absence wouldn't be felt as much. As she enters her preteen and teen years… that's when I definitely want to be around."

"I bet you're a good father, Gerald."

"I try." He reached for his coffee. "What about you? I know how dedicated you are to your career, but you never thought about marriage and motherhood?"

"I did once," Faye answered, picking up her orange juice and taking a drink. "I had a huge crush on you."

Gerald almost spewed hot coffee. "What?"

"That's right," Faye said, laughing. "When you arrived in Africa, I thought you were the man!"

"You're kidding." Faye shook her head. "I never would have known."

"I was too scared to tell you."

"Why?"

She reminded him about her experiences with Jesse and Phillip. "Guess you could say I was twice bitten, and when it came to expressing my feelings, very shy. Besides, it was obvious that you looked at me like a sister. Considering what happened, everything probably worked out the way it was supposed to."

"Or maybe that's what's happening now." Faye's look was questioning. "I did a little research before I came here. I'm very impressed with what you were doing in Haiti. I'd heard of the Haitian Heartbeats organization. In fact, I almost volunteered right after the quake myself."

"Why didn't you?"

"That country wasn't the only thing falling apart. The first of many cracks began appearing in my marriage around that same time."

"I'm sorry the marriage didn't work out."

"So am I. But it is what it is." Their meals arrived and they began eating. "So you used to have a crush on me, huh?"

Faye nodded. "Big-time."

"I actually liked you, too."

"No way!"

"I did." Gerald admitted with a nod. "But I didn't think you were interested. But that was then. This is now. And right now I'm both available and I'm interested."

Faye was floored. But she hid her surprise and confusion under a playful veneer. "Careful, Doctor. I'm not sure I'll allow fraternizing at my center."

"Well, in that case, I just might not take the job."

Faye sat back and eyed Gerald closely. "I'm sure you figured out that I'm dating Dexter, the man you met."

"I spent all evening trying to figure that out."

"When we started seeing each other, no one was more surprised than me. But don't judge a book by its cover. There's more to him than designer duds."

"He's not right for you."

"You don't even know him."

"I don't have to; I can look and tell." Faye remained quiet. Gerald continued. "Does he support your work at the center?"

"Yes."

"Understands and is okay with the dedication our profession demands, the time you're going to have to put into this job?"

"I think so."

"Make sure that he does. Because I can tell you from experience, if they don't understand, there is no way the relationship will survive."

Chapter 31

Before the clinic opened, Faye had thought she was busy. But now, less than a month after the Hearts of Health and Healing Center opened its doors, "not enough hours in the day" took on a whole new meaning. Sixteen-hour days were common. She was back to four or five hours of sleep. There were sick children, concerned mothers and need everywhere. Faye was exhausted but delirious with happiness. She was back in her element. This was her dream!

There was just one problem. Dexter. They'd only been together twice since the clinic's grand opening. The last time he'd come down she'd been too exhausted to do anything but sleep. He said he understood, but his actions told a different story. For the past week her calls had gone to voicemail. For all she knew, he'd given up and moved on. He was probably whizzing Erin Bridges around in that college fund he called a car or dancing the night away with any one of the women he'd charmed at Papa Dee's party.

And all of that would have been fine except for the fact that he had her heart in his pocket.

How did this happen? Even after that night following the grand opening and the talk that finally gave the term *relationship* to what they shared, Faye had vowed that she would not get caught up. She didn't have any problem with monogamy—heck, she could barely keep one randy man satisfied—but it still felt as if she was trying to please two lovers. One, Dexter. The other, the Hearts of Health and Healing Center.

Faye's intercom beeped. "Dr. Buckner, it's Adeline on one."

"Thanks, Vickie." Faye smiled, happy to hear from her friend. Dexter's no-show at the benefit had left Adeline totally unimpressed and underwhelmed, but the check and construction work he'd had donated had returned him to the "possible" category. Maybe Adeline could help figure out how to juggle these two demanding areas of her life. Faye walked over and closed her office door, then took the call off hold. "How did you know that I needed a pow-wow with my sister-friend?"

"You know we Haitians are spiritual," Adeline replied. "We know things."

"Okay, Ms. Spiritual. Since I assume you have a direct line to the All-Seeing, All-Knowing, please tell me what I'm supposed to do with this spoiled, stubborn man!"

"Hmm, a little trouble in your Southern California paradise with that fine brother?" After not meeting him when she visited California, she'd put his name in a search engine and found a picture online. But this was only after he returned to her proverbial good graces.

"You could say that." Faye gave Adeline an update, ending with the fact that she hadn't talked to Dexter in a week. "A part of me wants to just let him go so I can focus on the clinic."

"Don't you dare."

"But the other part really misses him, dang it. I don't want to miss him, Addie. I don't have time for screwy emotions like this!"

"Well, you'd better make time, Faye, because those screwy emotions are part of what we call life! I'm honestly happy to hear that you're feeling this way, girl. It means you're in love."

"No, I'm not." Adeline laughed but said nothing. "Yes, I'll admit that I enjoy our sex life. Quite a lot. Okay, almost as much as I love breathing."

"Ha!"

"But I already feel I made a mistake calling what we share a relationship. It demands too much of what I don't have."

"Such as?"

"Time! He wants to be with me, and I have to be at the clinic."

"You have to, or you think you have to because you think you're the only one who can take a temperature or wipe a brow? You told me about all the students who wanted to volunteer at your clinic, and about the retired nurses who are willing to come in for reduced pay."

Faye rolled her eyes and mumbled, "Obviously I've talked too much."

"In all the time I've known you, you've never mentioned a man. From everything you've told me about Dexter, he is pretty special. You know, before I met my husband, I was a lot like you, career-driven, believing that my professional accomplishments were enough. But my mother would always chide me—'Addie, those achievements aren't going to keep you warm at night. They're not going to comfort you when you're sick, and they won't cry for you when you die.' Take a step back, Faye, look at your life. Really look at it. What truly makes you happy, and what type of happiness does it bring? There are different kinds, you know." Faye remained silent. "I watched you pour your entire life into Haitian Heartbeats. That's well and good—if there are no other areas that need in attention in your life. There weren't any then, but there's someone now. So maybe it's time to reprioritize just a little bit. Faye?"

"I'm listening."

"Taking time for yourself doesn't take anything away from your commitment to helping others. Everyone who knows you knows how much you care. Maybe it's time to show that man of yours how much you care about him."

After a sigh, Faye responded. "Sometimes you get on my last nerve, Adeline Marceaux. And sometimes you're the lone voice of reason when I need it most. And all the time…you're my best friend. Thank you, sis."

"Thank me by getting off this phone and calling Dexter. And don't forget to let me know how it all works out."

Faye ended the call with Adeline, and before she could lose her nerve or change her mind, she dialed Dexter. Going over the message she'd leave in her mind, she was taken off guard when he answered.

"Dexter?"

"Isn't that the number you called?"

"I was expecting to leave a message."

"You want me to hang up so you can call back and do that?"

"Look, if you're going to act like an ass, then I can hang up and don't need to call back at all!"

"Whoa. I was just messing with you, baby. Sounds like somebody has some pent-up frustrations that need to be released."

"It is frustrating when one's phone calls aren't returned. Especially when they've been made to someone who was so adamant in defining our friendship as a relationship. It seems like ever since that happened, you've been unavailable."

"Me? Unavailable? You sure that's the limb you want to climb out on?"

"I'm too tired to climb or argue. I'm calling because I miss you, Dexter. Work has been crazy. And while I've been very upfront about the demands of establishing this center, I perhaps haven't been as vocal about how much I want you to continue to be a part of my life."

There was a long moment of silence before Dexter responded. "Okay."

"That's it? Okay?"

"I didn't know how you felt, Faye. It was clear that you cared about what happened to your center but not so much about what happened to us."

"Is that why you haven't returned my phone calls?"

"I got your messages. I could have called you. But a lot has been going on in my life, too." A pause and then. "Diamond had her baby."

"Oh, my goodness! The first child of the next generation. I'm so happy for all of you."

"Thank you. We're pretty happy, too."

"What did she have?"

"A boy. His name is Deval. Deval David Jackson Drake-Wright."

"Wow. Quite a name. Sounds like a lot of expectations are on his tiny shoulders."

"He's a Drake. He can handle it." A beat and then, "I missed you, too."

"You have?"

"Of course."

"Then why are you on the phone and not burning up the miles between us in that rocket you call a car?"

"My upscale Honda?" Faye was glad to hear the smile in his voice. "The center is closed on Sundays, right?"

"Yes."

"So why don't I arrange for a car to pick you up, get out of the urban oasis and relax for a minute, spend the night in wine country."

"I don't know, Dexter. Your mother is very astute. As much as I think I have your family's favor, I'm not too sure how she'd feel with her son's lover spending the night under the same roof as her."

"It's a really big roof," Dexter explained. "If it will help matters, no one even needs to know that you're in the east wing."

"But I'd want to stop by and see Papa Dee."

"Then you'll have to come out of hiding, my love." When Faye didn't object, Dexter continued. "I'll have a car there in a half hour. No need to pack much. We'll be naked most of the time."

Chapter 32

A few hours later, Dexter knocked on the door of the same suite Faye had occupied when she was first a guest at Drake Wines. He had one word for her as soon as she opened the door. "Chicken."

"Call me what you want," Faye said, turning around to give Dexter a full view of the snug shorts she wore. "But I didn't feel comfortable with the thought of sexing it up in your parents' house. I don't care how large an estate it is."

Dexter reached her in two strides and pulled her back against him. He began kissing her neck while his hand ran a trail from her breast to the valley of his temptation. Until meeting Dexter, to go from zero to sixty degrees of passion in nanoseconds was not something Faye thought possible. She turned and wrapped her arms around his neck. "I've missed you so much, Dexter." Kisses punctuated every word.

"Really?" He began his own exploration of her face with his mouth. "I couldn't tell."

"You know my schedule." Faye ran her hands over his shoulders and back.

Dexter grabbed her booty. "I'm getting ready to know this." He picked her up and walked them to the couch in the suite's sitting area. Soon, words gave way to a totally different kind of conversation. Faye relaxed into Dexter's arms and absorbed his kisses. When his hand once again slid toward the juncture of her paradise, she opened her legs to ease his access. No matter their differences in lifestyle, their crazy schedules or time apart, their lovemaking never suffered. Dexter had awakened a passion that Faye had never known. He'd awakened in her a sexual hunger that only he could satisfy. She put all else out of her mind except this man and this moment as she eased her hand inside his unzipped cargo shorts, searching for and finding a thick, hardened dick, fairly pulsating in her hand. She lightly ran a fingernail around the perfectly formed mushroom tip and was rewarded with a prolonged hiss. Emboldened, she slid off Dexter's lap and placed her face where her hand had been, taking him in, swirling her tongue around his member and causing his hips to begin a circular rotation to the beat of her strokes. She felt his hands in her curls, massaging her upper head while she massaged his lower one.

"Ooh, baby," he whispered, through clenched teeth after Faye produced a suction rivaling a vacuum cleaner. "Come sit on it."

Feeling powerfully seductive, Faye raised herself over Dexter's waiting manhood and slowly sank down before either of them thought about protection. The delicious friction created from this unexpectedly raw yet welcomed development caused them both to shudder. Over and again she performed this titillating act until Dexter, tired of the teasing, took her by the hips and took control. Pounding into her with powerful thrusts, he tossed his head back in ecstasy and concentration, and the world faded away save for the moist, soft body he held. Faye wasn't shy. She matched him stroke for stroke, encouraging him on like a jockey on a racehorse. "Yes!" she panted, using thigh muscles she didn't even know she had. "Ooh, feels so good. Yes! Like that! Oh!"

"Who does this belong to, huh?" Dexter's words were punctuated by thrusts, long and deep. "Whose is this?"

"Yours," Faye moaned.

"Say my name," he demanded, his thrusts more forceful, purposeful. In a sudden, unexpected move, he lifted her off him, sat her on the couch and stood behind her. Soon the heat of his sword was again felt inside her, and the dance resumed. "Say my name!"

"Dexter!" Faye was delirious with the pleasure he created. He churned. She chanted. "Dexter! Dexter! Dexter!"

Forty-five minutes later they sat at the dining room table, devouring the room service they'd ordered. "You can't make me wait this long no more," Dexter said around a crisp, hot fry. "You know if I don't get any, I'll go blind."

"Geez, Dexter, that is so lame." Faye savored a bite of her mushroom-topped burger. "You forget that you're talking to a doctor."

"Oh, right. Well, in that case it's not blindness. It's blue balls."

They continued in this teasing vein, and as much as she feigned irritation, she was secretly pleased to know that once again Dexter hadn't been with anyone during the time they'd been apart. Sometimes, as it was with the clinic, being with someone like Dexter felt like a dream. *When he can have his pick among all the women in California, what is it that he sees in me?* She decided to ask him.

Dexter finished his bite and sat back, his look thoughtful. "It's a number of things," he finally began. "First off, you're fine. No," he said, holding up his hand in anticipation of her protest. "You need to stop comparing yourself to the women you've seen around me or those Cali girls you see on the screen. Yes, they are beautiful, but so are you. There are different kinds of beauty. You've shown me a pure, simple beauty that I'd never noticed before but that I find quite attractive. You're not materialistic, nor easily impressed. You're smart. You're committed. And finally, you cast a mean line."

Faye smiled at his reference to her fishing abilities. "Don't forget how I handle a cast-iron skillet over an open flame."

"That, too." Dexter reached for his glass and finished off the lemon water. "Babe, what are you doing next Saturday afternoon?"

"You know what I'm doing on Saturdays. I'm at the clinic. Why?"

"One of my boys is having his thirtieth birthday party in L.A. I want you to come with me."

"Thanks, Dexter, but we're always so busy on Saturdays. Plus, LA is really not my scene."

Dexter's brows creased. "A free clinic isn't necessarily my scene, but that didn't stop me from coming and supporting you."

"That's different, Dex."

"How so?"

She turned to face him. "You honestly don't draw a line between saving lives versus shaking your rump?"

"It's not about the party, which is about more than butt shaking by the way. It's about being with me." He took a deep breath to calm his ire and tried to explain. "In my business, socializing, networking and scoring major contacts are all about business. High-profile clients staying here is great PR. Businessmen holding their conferences here is free marketing. One guy tells another how great it is, and before you know, the meeting rooms are booked year-round. There are going to be some A-list people at this party, and I have to tell you, it doesn't feel good having to explain the details in order to get you to come with me."

"I'm sorry, Dexter. I had no idea your attending this party had anything to do with business. I didn't mean to belittle you, or the invitation." She could tell he was still irritated. He had a right to be. "I'd love to come with you, but…"

He looked at her from the corner of his eye. "But what?"

"Gerald is coming into town next Saturday." Dexter huffed, but she decided to ignore his outburst. "He's taken a leave of absence from the hospital in Baltimore to do a thirty-day stint at the clinic. Depending on how all of that goes, he may relocate and become the second, much-needed doctor at the facility."

"When were you going to tell me that your long lost *friend* would be joining your staff?"

Faye took a calming breath before responding. "I'm telling you now."

"What does his being in town have to do with Saturday night?" Dexter asked, after several tense seconds passed.

"Pastor Jack and his wife, Millicent, have scheduled a dinner at their house with several of the board members, including one who is his neighbor and a millionaire, working in real estate."

"And you invited your doctor friend instead of me?"

"I didn't even think about you." Dexter jumped up from the table. "No," Faye continued, following him into the living room area. "Wait, that didn't come out right. I didn't think about inviting you because for Gerald, this is an informal interview. They'll have questions about his experience and he'll have questions about the clinic's ongoing funding, which will be how he gets paid."

Dexter stood with his back to her, staring at the back-lit fountain and pristine garden from the floor-to-ceiling windows in her suite. When she placed her arms around him and laid her head against his back, she could feel his tension. "You know, babe, this is all so new to me. You, this relationship, the health center, trying to balance it all. It's only been a few months. I'm still trying to figure it out, still learning about who you are and how you tick." She felt his muscles relax, felt his slow, deep intake of breath. "I care a lot about you, Dexter. Having you in my life has made me happier than I've ever been. You're important to me and I want to be with you and support you. I only hope that you can be a little patient with me until I can... figure it all out."

Instead of making love again, they talked for the next two hours. Dexter had a breakfast meeting and Faye was up and out of the suite before six the next morning. During the entire drive back to San Diego, she thought about what Dexter had said, how he supported what she was doing and how he understood.

But his parting hug—light and indifferent—had Faye questioning whether he would every really, truly comprehend the demands of her business. Had her thinking that maybe Gerald was right and that no one outside their profession could handle their demanding lives.

Chapter 33

"I can see myself living here in San Diego. It's nice." It was nine o'clock on Saturday night and Faye and Gerald were leaving the tony suburb of La Jolla and Pastor Jack Kirtz's ocean-view home.

"This area is certainly amazing," Faye agreed. "But you've got to have deep pockets to live here."

"Where do you live?"

"In an older, residential community not far from the center."

"The area around the clinic is a little shady. Is your neighborhood safe?"

"Most major city downtown areas have their questionable spots, but I'm about ten minutes from there and yes, I feel safe. There is a neighborhood watch group and I have nosy neighbors. Plus, mine is a security building."

"Any openings there?"

"You thinking about becoming my neighbor if you move?"

"Sure, why not?"

"There are only six units, and right now they're all rented. But I'll keep an eye out." She eased onto the freeway and continued. "One or two bedroom?"

"Probably three. One for my daughter, and one for my office/workout room."

"You can work out at our gym."

"That's true. But I'd still want an office." As they became silent, Gerald snuck glances at Faye's countenance. Something was bothering her; had been all night. She'd done her best to keep her smile bright and her voice lively, but he'd known her too long to be fooled. "Do you want to talk about it?"

"About what?"

"Don't even try it, Buck. We've shared too many secrets. I know when something's bothering you. If you'd rather not talk about it…"

"No, I don't mind. It may be good to get another male perspective."

"This must have something to do with your playboy."

"He's not a playboy, Gerald." Faye's tone showed her displeasure at his choice of descriptions. Forget the fact that at one time she'd called him that herself. She shared a bit of her conversation with Dexter. "He's my friend. And he's frustrated," she finished. "I don't blame him."

"I won't be the one to say I told you so."

"Look, there are millions of doctors who are practicing and also have stable, successful personal lives."

"Name five that you know of."

"That's not a fair question. You know that with the type of work I've done the past eight years, that most of those doctors are single. My best friend, Adeline, is no doctor. But she is a very dedicated administrator and the director of Haitian Heartbeats. She is also the mother of two, with a very understanding husband and support system. It is possible to have the best of both worlds."

Gerald eyed Faye a long moment. "Who are you trying to convince? Me...or yourself?"

While the ride back to Somerset Suites was quiet, the next day found Gerald and Faye sharing their usual camaraderie. After attending Pastor Jack's church service, they stopped at a seafood restaurant for Gerald's favorite: lobster.

"Are you still balking about trying this tasty crustacean?" Gerald asked, as they perused the menus.

"I don't want to bite anything that looks like it can bite me back."

"Then you should get it poached in butter without the shell. I guarantee you'll love it."

"I'm sure I would. But I think I'll have the blackened salmon over the wild rice pilaf." Faye took a sip of tea that the waiter had just put down.

"I'm excited that you'll be here for the radiology room construction." She went from lobsters to X-ray laboratories in the blink of an eye.

Gerald followed the transition effortlessly. "Are you still hoping for a digital imaging device?"

"You know I'd love one."

"But they're running, what...sixty, seventy thousand?"

"More like eighty."

"And the analogs are going for around twenty, twenty-five I'd imagine."

"Exactly."

"Is the construction firm that did the renovation going to do the install?"

Faye shook her head. "One of my contacts at San Diego State has recommended a company that specializes in these rooms. They're willing to do it at an extremely reduced fee because we're nonprofit."

"What are the specs?"

"Not sure yet." She looked at her watch. "But I need to know. I'll probably head over to the center after we're done here. I have a telephone conference with the guy next week."

"Would you like me to go with you?"

"Thanks, Gerald, but you've hardly seen the city. I don't want to encroach on your personal time."

"You know with a doctor there is no such thing. If you don't mind driving me around for one more day, I can skip going to the airport for my rental and go to the Hertz that's closer to the center on Monday."

"Sounds like a plan."

They finished their meal and headed over to the center. What was intended to be a five-, ten-minute stop to measure what would become the X-ray room turned into three hours of surfing the web for medical equipment and discussing the benefits of preventative and alternative health care. By the time she dropped Gerald off at his hotel and headed home, she'd forgotten all about calling Dexter.

And from the looks of the tabloid picture that greeted her the next morning when she stopped to get her morning coffee, he'd forgotten all about her, too.

Chapter 34

Faye pulled her Hyundai into the center's small parking lot and hurried inside.

"Good morning!" Vickie's sunny personality clashed against the storm inside Faye's heart.

"I need a minute," Faye said, passing Vickie's desk without stopping. "Hold my calls." She reached her office, closed the door and pulled out her cell phone. "I can't do this," was her greeting to Adeline.

"Good morning to you, too."

"Are you by a computer?"

"Yes. What's wrong, Faye?"

"Pull up a search engine and type in the name Maya Stone."

"Girl, I don't have to type that in an engine to know who you're talking about. I love her! That latest song she has out is the business!"

"No, her latest business is someone named Dexter. He

went to some swanky party over the weekend and now a picture of them all hugged up is splashed all over the tabloids!"

"What?"

"You heard me. The man who told me he wanted a relationship is out having relations."

"Okay, wait, Faye. Slow down. What did Dexter say?"

"Who cares what he has to say? That picture is worth a thousand words. No, just one—cheater." Faye, who'd sat down in one of the chairs facing her desk, now stood and began pacing. "I shouldn't even be mad, really. I knew what kind of man he was when I met him. I was fully aware of the consequences when I decided to have sex. Actually, I'm glad that I saw the picture. It's the cold water I needed to shake me out of the illusion that I could have someone like him and my career."

"Have you talked to him yet?"

"You know, Gerald is right."

"Gerald? As in McPherson? Your doctor friend?"

"His marriage ended because his wife just didn't understand."

"What does he have to do with this?"

"He's helping me out for thirty days."

"Excuse me, but why am I just hearing of this development?" Faye remained silent. "Helping...how?"

"Not in the way you mean. At the center. He's being considered for the director of urban modalities and outreach position. I'd remain director of clinical affairs."

"Wait, girl. You and your thoughts are all over the place. What is going on with you and Dexter?"

"Nothing, as of right now." Faye took a breath and told Adeline about hearing from Gerald, their conversation about possibly working together and finally about Dexter's friend's party and how she hadn't been able to attend because of her obligations to the center. "He just doesn't get it," Faye finished, plopping down in the seat behind her desk and swiveling around to face the window. "And I doubt he ever will."

"Looks like he's not the only one." Adeline's voice was soft, without judgment.

"What do you mean?"

"Look, you just said that the man invited you to a party where his attendance would be beneficial for his business. He asked you to go, which says a lot about how he feels about you. And it sounds like to me that you didn't understand the importance of his question and that you don't understand how things operate in his world. Yet you expect him to meld into your world seamlessly, to want what you want and to like what you like. You're pointing at him, Faye. But if I were you, I'd take a look in the mirror."

A long pause and then, "This is the second time in as many weeks that you've blessed me out."

"It's the second time that you've deserved it."

Faye smiled. "Just don't make it a habit."

"You stop acting like a brat and I'll stop acting like your mom." The women laughed. "How are you feeling, Faye?" There was a tinge of concern in Adeline's voice.

"I feel fine, why?"

"It's just that…oh, never mind. I guess I worry about you is all."

"Well, don't . I'm going to call Dexter just as soon as I get off with you. And thanks to our conversation, I won't be cursing him out as soon as he answers. If our relationship makes it, it will be in no small measure because of you."

"You can thank me by making me the matron of honor at your wedding."

"You're getting a little ahead of yourself."

"Maybe, maybe not."

"On that note, goodbye." Faye ended the call and dialed Dexter.

"Good morning, baby!"

"Good morning, Dexter. Sorry I didn't call you Saturday night. How was the party?"

"Crazy, but in the best of ways. My boy went all out for his thirtieth. Had Maya Stone in the house to sing him 'Happy Birthday.'"

"Yes, I know. I saw the picture."

"What picture?"

"You don't know? You're in a tabloid—front page."

"You're kidding."

"No, darling. You and Maya…well, let's just say it appeared you were having a very good time."

Five seconds passed. Ten. Two more. "It was all in good fun, babe. Nothing happened between her and me."

"Who says it did?"

"I have a sister and a mother and I know how women think." She could hear him clicking computer keys. "Oh, damn."

"Sounds like you found the picture."

"This looks bad. But I swear that all we did was talk and dance."

"I believe you."

"You do?"

"Yes. I'll admit this wasn't my first reaction. But after having time to think, *and talk to my bestie,* I realize that considering what you do and the circles you travel, pictures like these are bound to come up."

They talked for a few more minutes before Faye's first patient arrived. She was able to put the incident out of her head for the rest of the day. But as she headed for home and Dexter's visit, the tabloid was beside her, the picture was in her face, and she honestly didn't know if she could handle Dexter's lifestyle.

Her phone vibrated. She looked at the ID. *And then there's Gerald,* she thought as she pushed her hands-free device. As they chatted about various patients and events of the day, Faye found herself mulling over a serious question. Did she really want to live life in the fast lane? Or one as she'd have with Gerald, with a slower, more predictable ride?

Chapter 35

Faye and Dexter sat enjoying a meal at the home of Dexter's brother, Donovan. Or tried to anyway. "Dinner is delicious, Marissa. It really is. I just don't have much of an appetite. I haven't for the past few days."

"Do you think it's some type of stomach virus?" Marissa asked. "A woman at my job had it. She just came back today after being gone for almost a week."

"Working with sick kids every day, it could be anything. Eventually my resistance will build back up, but right through here I guess I need to be a bit more careful. I'll see how I'm feeling in the morning, and if I'm not any better I'll take an antibiotic."

Obviously neither Dexter nor Donovan had a problem with their appetites. Donovan paused just long enough to ask, "How is it going at the center?" before taking another bite.

"Really good, actually. Better than I expected."

"She's hired an old boyfriend to help her out," Dexter sniped.

"Not true," Faye replied. Marissa gave Dexter a chiding look then sent a sympathetic one to Faye. The Drake men were impressive, Faye mused, but she really liked the women in the family. "I worked with a doctor in Africa. He's taken a thirty-day leave from his job in Baltimore to help me get started."

"And to see if he wants to move here," Dexter added, sarcastically.

"Yes, there is another director's position being created, and he is being given serious consideration," Faye calmly explained.

"Dexter Drake. Is that a little bit of the green monster I see peeking over your shoulder?" Marissa reached for her wineglass and took a small sip.

"I'm not worried," Dexter tossed back. "Faye is in love with me. She isn't going anywhere."

"So sure of yourself?" Faye asked.

"Am I lying?" No comment. "I thought so."

"Don't mind Dexter," Donovan replied. "He was like this from the womb."

"Come on, Faye," Marissa said, rising from the table. "Help me with dessert in the kitchen. The chicken cacciatore might have been a little too spicy, but I think even a virus will enjoy this strawberry cake."

Dexter eyed Faye as she walked from the shower to the bed. "You should have had a second helping of Marissa's strawberry concoction. I think you're losing weight."

"I just haven't been hungry for a couple days." She climbed into bed and cuddled up next to Dexter. "And I have a fast metabolism. Don't worry. It's nothing. My weight often fluctuates when I'm stressed."

"Aw, is my baby stressed?" He positioned Faye in front of him and began massaging her shoulders. "Dang, baby, you are tight." He kneaded her neck and shoulders. "The center is running smoothly. What are you worried about?"

"We're supposed to remain objective, but sometimes I have a hard time staying detached from my patients. I treated a little boy today, four years old. He's grown up on a diet consisting mostly of fast food and soda and is suffering from type 2 diabetes as a result. Can you imagine? Diabetes? At four years old? Plus he's about twenty-five pounds overweight. If he keeps up his current lifestyle, he'll also be a heart patient before long. It's sad."

"You can't save the whole world, baby," Dexter said, kissing her ear. "Do your best and trust the universe for the rest."

She turned in his arms. "When did you become so prolific, Mr. Drake?"

"I've always been scholarly. I thought you knew?"

She swatted his arm. "You're a piece of work, you know that?" she asked with a laugh.

"I know. That's why you love me."

"Yes, Dexter, I love you."

His eyes widened in surprise. "Didn't think I'd admit it, huh? I'm kinda stunned myself. But somehow you've blown into my life much like a tornado and spun everything around. It's scary territory, but I can say it. I love you."

Dexter flipped them so that he was on top. "I love you, too."

The kiss was gentle, tender...once, twice, a third time. Leisurely, he acquainted his tongue with her soft, moist cavern; reverently he nibbled her upper and lower lip. Faye liked the pace and drew lazy circles across his bare back as she kissed him back. Their tongues lightly touched, his outlining her open lips before she pulled his bottom lip between her teeth. Their hips began a familiar grind. He moved down and eased her raisin-colored nipple into his mouth. She purred her pleasure, running her hands over his tight curls as his head went lower still.

He swirled his tongue against her navel. It tickled. She laughed and followed that with a quick intake of breath as his finger sought and found entry between her dewy folds. Farther down he continued until his lips met her nether pair. He kissed her there, slowly, deeply, flicking his tongue against her nub until it was a hardened pebble in her valley of love. After kissing a trail from her thighs to her toes and back, he entered her. The plunge was swift and powerful.

"Ah!"

"Uh-huh."

The dance began.

"Open your eyes," he commanded as he ground himself against her, pushed himself inside her so deeply that Faye felt she just might faint. She looked into eyes almost black with desire, not aware that Dexter was seeing the same. "I love you," he whispered, continuing to stare as he pulled out to the tip, plunged in again—out, in, side to side, stroking, grinding, loving her hard. Faye grabbed his buttocks and wrapped her legs around him. The sparks began deep within her core. The moans intensified as she felt a rush of sensations, felt her legs start to tremble as Dexter's stroking increased and his mouth went slack and they both went over the edge of ecstasy and crashed back down into a bed of spent love.

The next morning, Faye rushed to get ready while Dexter devoured a bowl of cereal in the dining room.

"You need to quit biting me," she said as she passed him on the way to the kitchen.

"Huh?"

"You heard me. Quit biting me. My nipples are sore."

"You weren't complaining last night."

She reached into the refrigerator for the orange juice. "I didn't feel it last night. I was too busy feeling...other things." She bent down and kissed his forehead before taking a seat across from him.

He finished the cereal and looked up. "You look better this morning."

"I feel better."

"Girl, you know if you're away from me too long, you get sick."

"I know you're about to make me sick right now."

"Ha!" Dexter put his bowl in the kitchen sink and headed to his phone on the living room coffee table. "Mama is scheduling a big party for Deval, so call me later. I want to let you know the date as soon as possible. Not attending is not an option. Trust me, you don't want to get on Genevieve's bad side."

"I wouldn't dream of missing your nephew's celebration." She walked him to the door. "I'll call you later."

By the time she arrived at the center, the grogginess that she'd felt upon waking had returned. *That's what you get for screwing half the night,* she scolded herself. Still, the lack of sleep was bringing with it a slight headache, and with the patient load she had today she needed to be at one hundred percent.

"Good morning, Buck."

Faye stepped fully into the break room. "Hey, Fear."

Gerald turned from the coffee machine. "You okay?"

"A little tired, but I'll be fine."

"Are you sure?" Gerald walked over and put a finger under Faye's chin. Her look was one of chagrin as she stared at him. "You look a bit ashen." He felt her neck. "A little bit of a temperature, too."

"I might take an antibiotic later. I have to make a phone call. See you later."

Faye reached her office and closed the door. Her mother had left a message the night before and Faye was determined to call her before the day started. Once the patients started coming in, other items on the day's agenda were often forgotten. "Hi, Mom."

"Well it's about time you returned my call." There was sarcasm in Mrs. Walker's voice. But also love.

"I'm sorry for not calling," Faye managed between yawns. "I've been so busy here. Getting little sleep and hardly no appetite. I think I've caught a bug."

"Or a baby," Mrs. Walker retorted. "You pregnant?"

Faye's head shot up. "Of course not."

The rest of the conversation went by in a fog. As soon as Faye got off the phone, she went and grabbed a pee cup. Ten minutes later, she got the results.

It was positive. Another Drake baby was on the way.

Chapter 36

"What is it, Faye?" Dexter sat in his west wing living room, watching Faye pace with growing concern.

"I don't know how to say it. I don't know how to tell you!" She'd carried on a conversation in her head during the entire drive up from San Diego. Now, all of those words seemed inadequate. This whole relationship thing wasn't going as planned, and neither was this conversation.

Is she getting to break up with me? If this has anything to do with Gerald McPherson I'm going to drive to San Diego and kick his—

"I'm pregnant." Faye looked at him then, her eyes wide and sad.

"You're...what?"

"I'm pregnant, Dexter."

"With a baby?"

"No," she deadpanned. "With a mule."

"I'm sorry." Dexter crossed the room to where Faye

stood. "I'm just shocked. I mean, you're a doctor. You knew we were rolling raw. I never even thought to ask about birth control. I mean…you're a doctor!"

"I know my profession, Dexter!" Faye shouted. "You don't have to remind me!"

"Well, obviously someone should have schooled you in a few things—at least remind the *doctor* where babies came from!"

Faye walked over to the couch, snatched her purse off it and headed for the door.

"Faye, wait." He grabbed her arm.

"Let go of me!" she hissed.

"We need to talk about this."

"I'm too upset to talk right now."

"I'm not going to let you drive away."

"I'm not going to let you keep me here."

Dexter leaned against the front door and crossed his arms. "Well, then it looks like we have a problem."

They gave each other the silent treatment for five whole minutes.

"My periods have been irregular for a very long time," Faye finally began, her words cutting through the living room's thick, weighty tension. "And I have a tilted uterus. A gynecologist told me years ago that I'd have a hard time getting pregnant." Faye thought back to how ferociously she and Dexter made love. "Guess he'd never heard about a Drake dick."

The slightest of smiles scampered across Dexter's face but was gone in an instant. "Do you want a baby?"

"Not really." Faye rubbed a weary hand across her forehead. "Don't get me wrong. I love kids. Just never thought about being a mother. Plus, the timing is all wrong. I just started the center and there's so much to do. How can I even think about dealing with a child right now?"

"I don't know what to say, baby. I'm shocked."

"Do you want a child?"

"I didn't think so." Dexter got up from the chair, walked over to a bar area and opened a bottle of wine. He poured the deep burgundy liquid through an aerator, watched as it ran through the sieve, listened as the device hissed and sputtered, reintroducing oxygen into the brew. "But then I met Deval, Jackson and Diamond's son. One look at that little man staring up at me and my heart melted." He looked over at Faye, who appeared deep in thought. "But I agree about the timing. You've just started the center. I'm going into business with my cousins in the north. There will be a lot on our plate over the next year."

"Plus we're not even married. I really don't want to be a single mother raising a child."

"It's actually kinda late for this conversation. The baby's on the way now. We'll just have to deal with it."

"There's always the option of—"

"No. There's not. We've created a Drake. You're getting ready to become one."

"What? Did I hear you correctly?"

"My parents aren't going to go for a Drake being born out of wedlock."

"Oh, so this is your idea of a wedding proposal?"

"No."

"Good, because as dry and unrehearsed as that statement sounded, you were getting ready to hear a solid 'no.'"

"Wait a minute," Adeline said, as muffled sounds came through the phone. "Sorry about that. I had to lose the kids and come into the bedroom because I could not possibly have heard you correctly."

As much as she didn't want to say it once let alone

twice, Faye repeated her opening statement. "Yes, you did. I'm pregnant, Adeline."

"Oh my goodness."

"Believe me, I'm in shock, too."

"Well, since meeting your man you have been doing the nasty almost non-stop and being a doctor, you had to realize this was how babies are made."

"Stop sounding like Dexter. This is all your fault!"

"I'm all the way over here in Haiti; how'd I do anything?"

"It was your idea for me to knock the cobwebs out of my cootchie!"

"Yes, but I didn't tell you to knock them out with an unshielded sword."

"It happened one night when we got carried away and because we were in an exclusive relationship by then, I didn't think anything of it. I especially didn't think about… this!" Her voice cracked as she continued. "Whenever Dexter's hard body is around me, I guess I never think much at all."

"Have you told him?"

"Yes."

"How'd he take it?"

"About like I did; surprised, not ready." She paused to grab a Kleenex; wiped her eyes and blew her nose. "I still can't believe I'm pregnant."

"I'm not totally surprised."

"What do you mean?"

"I could have told you that you were. I had a feeling."

"Yeah, right."

"I'm serious, girl. Remember that day you called me about seeing Dexter and Maya on that tabloid cover?" Faye nodded. "Remember when I asked how you were feeling?"

"You're always asking me how I'm feeling."

"This was different though. You said something and I got a feeling, deep in the pit of my stomach, the same way I did before my sister had her twins. You know I'm spiritual," she added after a beat. "I know things."

"Then I wish you'd known that one of Dexter's sperm had an upcoming play date with my egg so that I could have postponed it."

Silence, and then, "You don't want this baby, Faye?"

"Honestly? I don't know. I've never thought too much about it. Right now I've already got one baby named Hearts of Health and Healing in downtown San Diego. I don't know if I can handle another one right now."

"So you're thinking of terminating the pregnancy?"

Faye sighed. "Not really and even if I were, it's too late for that."

"How far along are you?"

"Not that far but it wouldn't matter. That option was off the table as soon as I told Dexter. His chest is all puffed out because he's created another Drake."

"Aw, that's sweet."

"Yeah. Whatever."

"It is! And I'm excited too. In about what, six or seven months Aunt Addie is going to have another baby to spoil!"

"This is madness," Faye continued, unmoved by Adeline's excitement. "Me and Dexter's relationship is still so new. Not even two weeks ago, I thought it might have ended. And now we're talking about having a baby together? It's madness," Faye repeated. "I haven't even considered being a wife; let alone a mother."

"Looks like life has made it more than a consideration. It's inevitable, Faye. You're going to be a mother. I suggest you get over the shock and start planning for a little one. And remember, what doesn't kill you makes you stronger."

"Are you sure?"

"Ha! Positive. Trust me; you'll take one look at that child and wonder how you ever lived without it."

Chapter 37

It had been more than a week since Dexter's world got turned upside down with the news that he was about to become a father. That first night after talking-slash-arguing with Faye he'd gone to the wine cellar, pulled out a bottle of premium vino and drank the whole thing while contemplating the dilemma her announcement had caused. On one hand, he cared a lot for Faye, was in love with her even. But did that mean he was ready for the ring, the kids, the white picket fence? On the other, what were his options? As soon as Genevieve Drake got wind of another baby coming, she'd be ordering a cake with a couple on top.

"Ah, man, what are you gonna do?" Dexter stood and began to pace, a common occurrence since trying to deal with this news all by his lonesome. Trying to handle this by himself without telling the family was almost as challenging as the situation itself. It was probably the only thing he'd kept from his siblings in twenty years. But this wasn't something he could tell one family member and not expect the whole clan to know within twenty-four hours. Or was there?

Twenty minutes later, Dexter was knocking on his great-grandfather's door.

"Make your entry and state your business," a gruff voice said from just inside the door.

Dexter smiled as he let himself in, already feeling better and surprised that he'd not thought of Papa Dee a week ago. "Hey, old man!"

"Watch yourself there, partner."

"You're not old yet?"

"You're as young as you feel, son. Charlotte's coming by to get me later so we can go play bingo. So tonight I'm feeling rather randy."

"Ha!" Dexter leaned down and kissed Papa Dee's forehead, then walked over and sat on the couch. He sighed heavily but said nothing.

"Where's that gal of yours?"

"Who?"

"What do you mean, who? That cute curly-haired gal you been courting."

Dexter shrugged. "At home, I guess."

"You guess? You don't know?"

"How should I know, Pops? I'm sitting right here!"

"Boy, don't get snippy with me in my own house!"

"Sorry, Pops."

"Ya'll have a fight or something?" Dexter shook his head. Papa Dee leaned forward and studied his favorite great-grandchild, noticing for the first time the tightness of his mouth and slight circles under his eyes. When he spoke, his concern was palpable. "What's going on with you, boy?"

"I've got a problem," Dexter admitted, with a shake

of his head. Papa Dee sat back, and waited for Dexter to continue. "Faye has gone and gotten herself pregnant."

"Another immaculate conception?" Papa Dee asked, his voice laced with subtle humor. Dexter fixed him with a puzzled look. "I'm thinking she must be the same as Mary was with the baby Jesus. Since she went and did this by herself."

"You know what I mean, Pop. It's mainly her fault."

"How you figure?"

"Because…she's a doctor! She knows how this stuff happens. I didn't think I'd have to—"

"Act like a man? Be responsible? Keep your pole wrapped up? It takes two to tango, son. Don't go blaming this on that gal. You're just as guilty."

"Yeah," Dexter said softly. There was no use arguing with his great-grandfather…or the truth. "I know."

"Well, boy, why you sitting there with your lip dragging so low you could trip over it? This is just life happening to you; nothing to be all sad about. You're getting ready to be a father; one of the best things that can happen in a man's life."

Dexter studied the faraway look in his great-grandfather's eyes. "You think so?"

"I know what I'm talking about. Holding David, Jr. for the first time was one of the best moments of my life. With every subsequent generation, life has just gotten better and better. Now little David will have a cousin to grow up with." Papa Dee nodded. "That's a good thing." The two men were silent for a moment. "So what are you going to do, son?"

"Take care of the baby," Dexter finally said.

"I'm not talking about the child," Papa Dee countered. "I'm talking about the doctor. When are you going to make an honest woman out of her?"

"I don't know, Pops," Dexter said with a sigh.

"Well, that bun will soon be baked and out the oven. So I suggest you best be finding out."

A few days after the conversation with Papa Dee, Dexter and Faye sat in the Grapevine's private dining room, having enjoyed succulent Maine lobster and chateaubriand.

"I didn't think I'd like it," Faye said, swirling a tender piece of claw meat in butter before plopping it into her mouth. "It's so rich, and tender. It almost melts in my mouth."

Dexter speared a piece of the tender beef. "Only the best for my baby mama."

"Do *not* call me that."

"Isn't that what you are?"

"I am an expectant mother, a pregnant woman or a woman with child. Once I deliver, I will be your baby's mother. Not a baby mama."

"All right." Dexter's eyes twinkled. "Baby mama." Before she could swat him, the waiter rolled in a tray laden with sweets. He pulled the cart up to them and then exited the room as quietly as he had come. "Didn't know what you'd want," Dexter explained. "Your appetite is all over the place these days." While Faye was distracted by the plethora of dessert choices, Dexter placed a ring box on the table.

"What's this?"

"Open it and see."

She slowly opened the black velvet box and pulled out a simply cut ring. "I love it," she said, examining the plain, white band. "You knew I'd want something simple. Is this ivory? Or bone?"

"Plastic."

Faye gave Dexter a look. "Oh, okay." She slid the ring

onto her left finger. Her eyes unexpectedly filled with tears. "Thank you."

"I haven't asked you to marry me, woman. Don't thank me yet."

"I didn't consider this an engagement ring," Faye responded. "I think it's pretty clear that marriage is the last thing that either of us wants."

Dexter was quite taken aback. It was one thing for him to feel that way and another to hear it, even though Faye's straight-forwardness was one of the things he loved most about her. "Are you telling me that you don't want to become my wife?"

"I don't want to get married just because we're expecting a child together. It's not enough to make a union last."

"It's not just the baby. I love you, too."

"Oh, now we're bringing up love."

"Dang, give me a break, Faye. This isn't easy."

"I know," she softly replied. "It isn't a walk in the park for me either." She reached across and placed a light hand on his arm. "I appreciate what you're trying to do, Dex. But this is the 21st century. Single women have babies every day."

"Not any single woman who's carrying my child," Dexter responded, a bit more harshly than he'd intended. "Faye, baby, I know this is coming out all wrong, that this sounds like my decision is all about the baby, and it's not. It's about you, and me, and this family I want us to have together. It's about me wanting to make a commitment; about me wanting to have a life that looks like my parents', and my grands', heck even my siblings'. Over this past week, I've done a lot of thinking. I've imagined what it would be like for me to be here, and you to be in San Diego…with our child. No matter how I envision the scenario…it doesn't feel good. I don't want to be a part-time father and more than that, I don't want to spend time in a household that doesn't include you. I know this is unexpected and there are challenges that we'll have to work out. But I think you and me together is a winning combination. Don't you?"

Faye's eyes shone with unshed tears. "You make it sound so easy," she whispered.

"It can be. Unless." Dexter's eyes narrowed. "There's somebody causing you to doubt us."

Faye shook her head. "You don't have to worry about Gerald. Sure, he's an old friend and I think of him fondly. But I'm in love with you."

"Does he know that?"

"Yes."

"And he's going to stay here knowing that there is no chance with you?"

Faye shook her head. "He's decided not to take the position, Dexter. He's gone back to Baltimore." Dexter visibly relaxed. "This time we've spent apart has been good for me, it's given me time to think about how my life would be without you in it. There's no doubt my world would be a much duller, dimmer place."

"So are you saying what I think you're saying?"

"What do you think I'm saying?"

"That you can't live without me?"

"You're so conceited."

"Yeah, but am I wrong?"

"No, you're not wrong."

"Um, baby," Dexter said, leaning over to place a tender kiss on Faye's lips. "There's something that sounds so right about that." He sat back down, and made a big show of patting his pockets, then pulled out another box. This one, blue.

"Dexter...what are you up to?"

"Go on. Open it."

Faye reached for the baby blue box. She opened the lid to reveal a silvery-colored metal box. Her brows creased as she pulled it out. "What is this?"

"Only one way to find out."

She lifted the lid. Her reaction was everything Dexter had hoped for as she viewed the diamond-encrusted, platinum eternity band that he'd had custom-made. Next to it was a plain, thin band. "Baby!" Faye walked to Dexter's side of the table and sat in his lap. "Sure of yourself much?"

Dexter laughed, running his hand up and down her silk-covered thigh. "I was hopeful." Faye gave him a look. "Okay, and maybe a little confident."

"This is so beautiful," she said, running her fingers over the ring. "But it's so flashy. I can't wear this in inner-city San Diego. What would those disadvantaged patients think?"

"They'd think you've got it going on!" he replied. "But I understand, which is why I added the plain band. That is for the doctor. This one is for my wife." He stood, sat her in the chair and got down on one knee. "Dr. Faye Buckner...will you marry me?"

"I guess I'll have to," she said as tears rolled down her cheeks. "Since I'm getting ready to be your baby mama."

Chapter 38

Three Months Later

"Faye? Are you back here?"

"Yes, Genevieve, I'm here!" Faye scooted toward the edge of the couch, holding the phone with one hand and balancing herself with the other. "Listen, Addie, that's Genevieve, my soon-to-be mother-in-law. They're probably waiting for me. I've got to go."

"Oh, I'm sorry, I didn't know that you were on the phone."

"That's all right. We were done talking." Faye barely heard Genevieve's chatter as they made their way from the east wing, where she and Addie had been talking, to the main dining room. She was too busy thinking about how drastically her life had changed since the pregnancy, and how it bore little resemblance to the one she'd imagined when landing at San Diego International Airport.

In the short time since she'd arrived in California, so much had happened: she'd met a man, fallen in love, moved to a condo, opened a clinic, gotten pregnant, gotten engaged, inherited a big family and in two short weeks would be moving into a beautiful home in suburban San Diego, just ten minutes from where Donovan and Marissa lived. If it weren't for the baby's constant kicks in her stomach—motions from a being that she hadn't yet seen but already loved more than she thought possible—she'd have to work hard not to believe that just like her first ride to the resort… this was all a dream.

Twenty minutes later, twelve people sat around Genevieve's dining room table. Having heard that it was Faye's favorite, they'd replaced their Creole standard with Mexican fare. Papa Dee was once again at the head of the table, looking as though he'd never been sick.

"I want to propose a toast to the latest generation, my namesake," he said, nodding at the portable crib just beyond the dining room. "Little David is going to take this place farther than all of us combined."

"It's Deval David, Papa," Diamond corrected for the umpteenth time. "De-VAL."

"I told you that first name sounded too much like Satan," he retorted. "Long as I live, the baby is going to be David to me." Various reactions from the table: smiles, twinkling eyes, a chuckle here and there.

"Now, I also want to toast the newest member of the family, Dr. Faye Buckner. You saved my life, gal. I want to thank you."

"You're very welcome, Papa Dee. It's what anyone with my knowledge would have done."

Papa Dee nodded toward Dexter. "And while you'll never get him to admit it, you saved his life, too."

"Thank you," Faye said amid the laughter, filled with

gratitude to have found such a wonderful family with which to belong. "Thank all of you."

With the toast over, a gentle mayhem ensued. Dishes were passed, silverware clanged and twelve people vied for their share of the conversation.

The deep voice of David Jr., Dexter's grandfather, cut through the din of chatter. "How are things at the clinic, Doctor?"

"Very well, Mr. Drake."

"That new doctor working out all right?"

Faye had to laugh at the thought of her sixty-something mentor, Dr. Ian Chappelow, who'd practiced medicine for forty years, being thought of as new. "We were blessed to get Dr. Ian on such short notice. When Dr. McPherson decided against taking the position—" Faye ignored Dexter's snort "—I was really at a loss. That Dr. Ian would spend the last year before he retired at the clinic he helped found is a godsend beyond my dreams."

Dexter, Donald and Genevieve were especially quiet. In time Faye would know of the part they played in getting Dr. Ian to come to San Diego, along with the immeasurable assistance of Adeline Marceaux.

"You never told us about the proposal, dear," Genevieve asked once she'd heard another second of silence wherein to slip the question. "Was Dexter's question a creative or common one?"

"You might say common," Faye said, enjoying the surprised faces, "considering he gave me a plastic ring."

"What?" Genevieve's hand went to her mouth.

"Plastic?" Dexter's father, Donald, said with a scowl.

"Boy," Papa Dee chided, "you were raised better than that."

"Yes, plastic," Faye continued. "At first. And then he

gave me this one." She held out her hand with the sparkling eternity band. Everyone approved.

"I can't even believe y'all tripped like that. You know there's nothing cheap about me. I'll never give my wife anything but the best."

"Promise?" Faye asked, exaggeratingly batting her eyes.

"Absolutely," Dexter said, with a nod. "And not a plastic promise either. I'll give you nothing short of a platinum promise, baby, rare and precious...just like our love."

"Now you're talking like you've got some datgum sense," Papa Dee said, still fixed on the absurdity of any Drake man offering a woman plastic jewelry, joke or no. "Now go on and give her a good old smooch." When Dexter hesitated, Papa Dee continued. "Go on. You got a seed growing in that there belly." He cocked his head at Dexter. "Don't try and act like you don't know how."

The wise, one-hundred-year-old patriarch had a point. He demanded that the lovebirds seal their love with a kiss. So they did.

* * * * *

Two classic Eaton novels in one special volume...

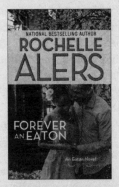

FOREVER
AN EATON

NATIONAL BESTSELLING AUTHOR
ROCHELLE ALERS

In *Bittersweet Love*, a tragedy brings history teacher Belinda Eaton and attorney Griffin Rice closer when they must share custody of their twin goddaughters. Can their partnership turn into a loving relationship that is powerful enough to last?

In *Sweet Deception*, law professor Myles Eaton has struggled for ten years to forget the woman he swore he'd love forever—Zabrina Cooper. And just when Myles is sure he's over her, Zabrina arrives back in town. As secrets are revealed, can they recapture their incredible, soul-deep chemistry?

"Smoking-hot love scenes, a fascinating story and extremely likable characters combine in a thrilling book that's hard to put down." —RT Book Reviews on SWEET DREAMS

Available May 2013 wherever books are sold!

HARLEQUIN®
™ www.Harlequin.com

KPRA1260513

REQUEST YOUR FREE BOOKS!

2 FREE NOVELS
PLUS 2 FREE GIFTS!

KIMANI™
ROMANCE

Love's ultimate destination!

KROM13R